VALLEY OF
DRY BONES

AN ARKANE THRILLER
J.F. PENN

Valley of Dry Bones. An ARKANE Thriller Book 10
Copyright © J.F.Penn (2018). All rights reserved.

www.JFPenn.com

ISBN: 978-1-912105-17-5

Requests to publish work from this book should be sent to:
joanna@CurlUpPress.com

Cover and Interior Design: JD Smith Design

Printed by KDP Print

CURL UP
PRESS

www.CurlUpPress.com

"And as I was prophesying, there was a noise, a rattling sound, and the bones came together, bone to bone. **8** I looked, and tendons and flesh appeared on them and skin covered them, but there was no breath in them.

9 Then he said to me, "Prophesy to the breath; prophesy, son of man, and say to it, 'This is what the Sovereign Lord says: Come, breath, from the four winds and breathe into these slain, that they may live.'" **10** So I prophesied as he commanded me, and breath entered them; they came to life and stood up on their feet—a vast army."

Ezekiel 37: 7-10

"The past is not dead. In fact, it's not even past."

William Faulkner

PROLOGUE

Guinea, Africa. 1731

THE SCREAMING DIDN'T STOP until just before dawn.

Miguel Rey huddled underneath one of the mud huts, his face pressed into the dirt. The smell of blood hung in the air, a coppery tang over the acrid pall of smoke from the burning roofs of the village. Miguel's arms ached from the pressure of holding his hands over his ears, the futility of trying to shut out the agonized cries of the dying.

He should have been one of them.

The raiding party had come in the small hours of the night, easily overpowering the outer guards, running through the village. Some of the raiders carried shackles, others carried machetes, and each went about his work with no hesitation.

There were strong men in the village, and women of childbearing age – all worth a great deal as slaves, for it was not only white men who stole black gold. It was usually rival tribesmen who raided villages in the interior, driving their captives back to the coast where slavers would take them west to the New World.

Miguel had watched from the shadows as knives slashed

and women were beaten to the ground even as the villagers fought back against the invaders. He clutched the cross around his neck, wondering whether the Lord called him to martyrdom.

Then he ran, hiding under the hut, a mute witness to the savagery.

When silence eventually fell, Miguel wondered if there would be anyone left. Would he die here in Guinea, the last of his missionary party?

When he first arrived here two years ago, Miguel had stumbled out of the forest, his legs weak from fever, his guts infected by parasites, his mind already in another realm. The villagers cared for him, as Jesus told his followers to do. The village shaman gave him foul-tasting herbal concoctions to drink – perhaps it was *ekong*, witchcraft, or perhaps the Lord's blessing in disguise – but Miguel was soon back on his feet. Even the disease of bony growths on his body that had plagued him since childhood were gone after the shaman had finished his work.

It was a good and simple life, and Miguel quickly became part of it. He sat talking with the men, ate cassava root with them, supplemented by duck or even red river hog when the hunters got lucky. He celebrated the birth of their children by drinking palm wine. He struggled to learn the language, but the villagers were gentle, coaxing him into learning the names of various plants. They had been his friends.

Miguel came to bring the gospel to a heathen people, but instead, he discovered those whose faith and good works challenged his own. They were not people of darkness, they were children of God.

Now Miguel lay motionless in the dirt, listening for a sound that might indicate any were left alive.

He lay there until the sun rose higher, until it was clear that the raiders had gone. When all was silent, he crawled out from beneath the hut and brushed dirt from the robe he still wore as a priest of the Catholic Church.

Miguel crept toward the center of the village, where the fire pit acted as a central meeting place, where the villagers usually sat talking or sharing a common meal. The coo of a blue-headed wood dove called softly from the surrounding kapok trees as he stopped in the shadows of one of the huts and peered around the corner. He clutched a hand over his mouth in horror.

Bodies of the villagers not taken by slavers lay strewn across the ground, some curled in the fire pit, burned beyond recognition. Others slashed with deep machete wounds. Crimson stains pooled on the dusty earth beneath them, drying in the rays of light that dawned on good and evil alike. The air reeked with the stink of burned flesh. Miguel felt his gorge rise and swallowed down bitter bile as he took a step out, eyes fixed on the dead.

The sound of footsteps.

He darted back to the shadows, making sure he was hidden before peering around again.

The old shaman shuffled out from behind the trunk of a tree. His wrinkled face usually wore a broad smile, but now his eyes were sunken, his mouth twisted in pain as he carried the weight of grief upon him.

The shaman bent to one of the bodies, then straightened, lifting his hands to the sky, his mouth moving in a whisper. He pleaded with the ancestors, with the spirits of the trees around him, and with the gods of this land, to release the dead to the next world.

But as he moved amongst the bodies, the shaman's face transformed from one who accepted death to one determined to overcome it.

He bent down to a little girl with a deep bloody wound across her neck, then rose to his full height, eyes like thunder as he stared up at the storm clouds gathering above. The shaman shook his head in determination, clenched his fists and strode into his hut.

Miguel crept forward to the doorway, desperately wanting to know what the man was going to do.

"I see you, priest." The deep voice came from within. "Enter and witness the wrath of my ancestors."

Miguel walked inside, his legs shaking as he met the shaman's dark eyes. The old man seemed suddenly taller, as if his physical frame was just a shell for the powerful spirit within. Shadows weaved about his body as he spoke.

"A great darkness came upon this land when the white men landed. My brothers sell their own for gold. But those they killed here will not rest in peace. They will rise up and slaughter those who wronged them. They will not stop until they bring to justice those who kill their children, enslave their women and carry their young men across the ocean to a foreign grave."

The shaman bent to the racks of carved wooden boxes full of ingredients at the back of the hut. Miguel had thought these to be simple herbal remedies, but now doubt flooded his mind.

The shaman reached behind the boxes and pulled out five small ivory horns, each hollowed out to create a kind of vial, each plugged with beeswax. He carried them to the hearth along with a large bowl, then reached for a bottle gourd. The shaman took a swig, gulped it down and offered it to Miguel.

"Drink this. You're going to need it if you want to witness the Breath."

Miguel had always resisted the shaman's drink before, fearing its potency, but this time he accepted it and drank deep. The liquid was sweet and cloying, sticking to his throat, pungent with the scent of buried roots and honey. Within moments, he felt a sensation of lifting away from his body, colors growing stronger as his focus shifted.

The shaman began to chant as he mixed the powder from the horns into the bowl, using liquid from the gourd to dilute it until a thick brown paste remained. He stood up and carried the bowl outside to where the slaughtered bodies lay.

Miguel followed him back out into the sun, shielding his gaze from a world dialed up in sensation. Flies buzzed around the bodies, landing on gaping wounds and open, staring eyes. The brilliant red of blood, the intense green of trees around him, the heady scent of flowers over the stink of gore, the hot sun on his skin. It sank into his soul, searing his mind, and Miguel wondered if he would ever be able to forget what he saw this day.

The shaman began to chant a refrain, a prayer to the ancestors, an invocation to bring the fallen warriors home again. Even with Miguel's basic knowledge of the local language, he could still recite phrases, and now he repeated the lines over and over – something about the four winds breathing into the slain. He found himself chanting along with the shaman, and perhaps in the depths of his soul, he called to his own God, a common humanity across the cultural divide.

The shaman walked around the bodies, dabbing paste from the bowl onto the lips of the dead. He marked their foreheads with a symbol, curving lines of the breath of the divine, the spirit of the ancestors. He continued chanting until every single body had the mark and each corpse was anointed with the paste.

When he had finished, the shaman sat down heavily on the ground by the fire pit. He shrank into himself, almost as if his body desiccated under the sun, as if he had poured his own strength into them all. Then the old man wept, his tears soaking the earth, pooling with the blood beneath.

Miguel felt his own eyes prick with tears at the loss of the villagers he had grown to love. It was the end of his life here in Africa, for there was only one way forward for him now.

Suddenly, a mighty wind swept through the kapok trees, rustling the leaves and sending the birds to flight.

Dark clouds gathered above, whirling into a vortex where lightning flashed, illuminating winged creatures with forked tails. As Miguel stared up at them, unsure of what he really saw, the ground trembled beneath him.

He stumbled and fell to the ground. When he looked up again, the creatures were just clouds moving and shifting in the wind. The tremor passed as quickly as it had come and then it was quiet once more.

Miguel took a long deep breath, anchoring himself with the rough feel of the dirt under his hands. The shaman's potion must have –

A sudden movement caught his eye.

Miguel turned his head. What was that? His heart beat faster. Maybe the raiders had returned.

Another twitch.

It was one of the dead women near the fire. Her hand moved, fingers clutching the air. But it could only be a trick of the light or some animal gnawing at her broken body, desecrating the corpse.

Miguel rose to go and get rid of it, but as he moved nearer, he could see nothing by her body. He frowned and bent down to look closer.

The dead woman turned her head.

Miguel let out a small cry, stepping back in horror. Her eyes were cloudy, opaque, as if a veil had fallen down over them. He put his hand out. "Agnes?"

She bared her teeth and snarled, her fingers curling into claws. Miguel jumped back in alarm. This was not the Agnes he once knew.

The shaman clambered to his feet, hope in his eyes. "The gods have answered."

Other villagers began to sit up, oblivious to their deep bloody wounds, eyes empty. The shaman walked around to each one, calling his thanks to the ancestors above for bringing them back from the dead.

But they were not back, not really.

"What have you done?" Miguel called out.

The shaman looked over, his eyes red-rimmed. "I have unleashed the dead on those who wronged them. Run, priest. You have no home here anymore."

The shaman turned back to minister to his army of the dead.

Miguel put his hand to his forehead, closed his eyes, wondered if this was all a vision from the potion he had drunk. But then he looked again at those around him. The dead had truly returned from the grave. Or at least some semblance of them. Was this black magic, or was this the revelation of the Breath as recounted by the prophet Ezekiel?

An idea began to form.

An army of the dead was a precious gift that could be used for the expansion of empire. A gift that would ensure his future.

As the shaman ministered to his new followers, Miguel slipped back to the hut. He gathered up the five horns, stopping each with wax again. He wrapped them with sacking and put them into a woven bag along with water and provisions for his journey. The nearest trader town was two days' walk away, and from there he would get on a boat and head north to Europe.

This secret could change everything.

CHAPTER 1

New Orleans, USA. Present day.

AS THE RAIN THUNDERED down for the seventh night, water seeped through the earth, trickling through the soil, widening the cracks. It curved over tattered remains of the dead and around the carapaces of scuttling things with unseeing eyes.

The chamber had remained hidden for so long, but finally, darkness awakened, a fissure opened.

A grave fell inwards from above, collapsing into the pit. The clouds shifted, and a shaft of moonlight pierced the gloom. Shadows whirled, awoken at last, as rain trickled toward the dry bones.

* * *

As dawn light filtered through the broad branches of the southern live oak, Luis Rey stood underneath a black umbrella watching his men as they widened the fissure leading into the tomb, making it safe to descend. The rain pattered down, a drumbeat that matched his racing heart as he leaned over his ebony walking cane, twisted fingers gripping the bone handle. Could this really be the place after all these years of searching?

Sweat trickled down his spine, the heat oppressive even at this early hour. Generations of his ancestors had lived in the Deep South, but something in his blood pined for the cool heights of the Sierra Nevada, the mountains of Andalusia. Yet his family would never leave this place, not without the Hand of Ezekiel. Luis trembled at the thought of what lay beneath. Could he be the one to find it?

In the center of the bustling city and yet removed from it by high walls and superstition, the St Louis Cemetery No. 1 was packed with vaulted tombs built above ground to protect them from flooding. The stone tombs housed the dead from the great families of the past, names etched into history as witness to the changing city. Some carvings had faded with time, the edges of tombs crumbling as the grey stone weathered away. Others were lime-washed white with detail in bronze. Angels with wings spread wide loomed over the graveyard – a hope of protection in the darkness beyond. How little they knew of suffering, Luis thought as he looked out over the cemetery.

But they would find out soon enough.

With the help of a local councilman encouraged by generous donations, Luis had surveyed the cemetery multiple times over the years, using the ever-shifting earth as an excuse for his private quest. It made sense for the chamber to be here. After all, the cemetery had been built after the great fire that destroyed much of New Orleans in 1788 – a fire that his family journals claimed to have been started as a way to destroy the Hand of Ezekiel relic forever. But they had never given up the search.

Luis had used ground-penetrating radar to search underground without disturbing the tombs above, but there had never been anything to investigate further, nothing that might have pointed to a hidden chamber.

But something had changed last night. Something shifted under the earth, and he could only dare to hope it was what he sought.

"Señor," Julio shouted, pushing back the hood of his yellow rain jacket with a muscled arm as he waved with excitement. In all their years of working together, Luis had never seen his bodyguard's eyes light up this way. But then he was more than just muscle. Julio was a man of true faith, committed to the cause, whatever it might take.

The team of workers around him moved back, revealing a way down.

Luis shuffled toward the hole, sensing movement in the darkness below. While his mind raced ahead, his limbs moved with agonizing slowness as he took each painful step.

Born with a rare connective tissue disease, Fibrodysplasia ossificans progressiva, it slowly turned his muscles, tendons and ligaments to bone. It was daily agony, but Luis understood that the Lord had blessed his family with the affliction. It kept their focus on searching for the relic over generations, reminding them of the sacred task with daily physical awareness. He thanked God for it, even as his bones ground against each other and he dragged his twisted limbs onward. Perhaps his reward was finally within reach.

Some of the men turned their eyes away from his contorted form, but Julio's gaze never wavered. He didn't shrink from suffering. His family had been in service to the Reys for almost as long as the Spanish had been in the New World. Their families were bound together, an ancient blood pact that together they might finally end.

Luis stepped to the edge of the hole. Julio reached for his arm, helping him to bend and look inside. "Could this be it?" he whispered.

Luis nodded. "Perhaps." He leaned forward, but he could see only collapsed stone and darkness beyond. It smelled of fresh rain and the mulch of pungent earth with a note of sulfur beneath. "I need to get down there."

"It's not safe yet. Wait until we rig some ropes."

Luis looked up at Julio, his jaw set, his dark eyes almost black in the dawn light, a promise of future rage.

Julio took a step back, biting his lip. "Of course. Right now. I can help you down myself." He turned to the workers. "Stay back. Don't stress the ground. But be ready with ropes just in case."

He picked up a head-lamp and put it on, slinging a pack with safety gear onto his back.

Julio stepped down onto the rubble of the tomb, lifting up his arm as support. Luis placed his walking cane carefully down onto the first stone and took his first step.

"Stop in the name of the Lord!"

A tall, thin man stepped from the shadows behind a tomb. He wore a brown monk's habit, tied simply at the waist with a piece of rope, the hood up obscuring his features. A heavy bronze crucifix hung around his neck.

"You trespass against God in this place."

The man's voice was deep and slow, like the languid movement of the waters in the Louisiana bayou. He pushed his hood back, revealing pale skin and grey eyes that echoed the stone of the tombs around them. His flesh hugged tight against his skull, his head shaved close and nicked in places, leaving patches of dried blood. He looked as if he subsisted on air alone.

The monk strode toward the hole, his right fist clenched around the crucifix.

The workers drew back, eyes looking away, unwilling to challenge a holy man. Some of them crossed themselves as he passed.

Luis stood his ground, Julio holding strong beside him, as the monk pushed to the edge of the hole.

"What right do you have to desecrate this holy ground?"

Luis tilted his head to look up at the monk. "The right of my ancestors who have sought this place for generations."

The monk's eyes widened. "Then you are–"

His words were cut off as Julio grabbed the monk and forced him to his knees. He tried to shout but the noise was muted by the stone and the rain and the rag they stuffed in his mouth.

Luis looked down at the monk kneeling before him. "Push his head forward."

The man struggled, but Julio pushed him down and pulled down the robe revealing a stylized tattoo of wind swirling around a cross of bone on the base of his neck.

Luis spat in the monk's face, barely hearing the audible gasp from the men around him. "You are Brotherhood of the Breath, one of the traitor Père Antoine's bastard breed. But it ends here. Your very presence confirms this is the true resting place and your sacrifice will begin a new cycle." Luis stepped away. "Bind him and lower him down." He looked out at the wakening city. "Then guard the perimeter. No one must come down here until we are finished."

Julio's men wound guide-ropes around the monk and lowered him into the darkness. When the rope went slack, they threw the end in after him. Luis began the slow journey down, relishing each step on the stones of history as Julio helped him climb into the chamber.

When they reached the bottom, Luis paused for a moment, listening to the darkness. Was there a faint rattling, like bones against a casket?

The moans of the bound monk echoed around the chamber, the sound revealing a bigger place than expected. Luis shook his head. There was no way he could have missed this with the radar. It was as if it had appeared overnight, some opening into another world that slipped through the shadows of time.

Julio unpacked his bag, bringing out stronger lights. He flicked on a powerful flashlight and shone it around the chamber, his hand shaking a little as it revealed what lay ahead.

The floor was layered with bones, some full skeletons with rusted swords in their hands, some arranged in intricate designs, others piled high like a mass grave. Julio crossed himself as he raised the light higher. Pelvis bones and femurs lined the walls while a ceiling of skulls gazed down with empty eyes.

"We need to go deeper. The Hand of Ezekiel must be here." Luis took the flashlight from Julio and started forward, shrugging back at the bound monk. "Bring him."

Luis walked on, his thin ray of light lancing through the darkness, illuminating the long dead, their dull-white bones reflecting the glow back at him. Julio walked behind, carrying the bound monk, and together they formed a slow procession toward their final goal.

An altar made from criss-crossed leg bones fused with skulls and on top, a casket made from tiny bones fitted and fused together, inlaid with exquisite gold filigree.

Luis exhaled slowly and walked to it, putting his hand on what his family had sought for generations. Was there a vibration from inside, or did he imagine it? His heart pounded in expectation at what lay within.

The monk twisted and moaned more loudly as Julio dropped him on the floor near the altar.

Luis leaned closer.

He opened the lid and gasped. "No, this can't be right."

Inside, there was only a faded crimson silk cushion with five compartments, empty of the relics he so desperately sought.

Luis spun around and ripped the gag from the monk's mouth. "Where is it?"

The monk laughed with triumph. "You will never find the Hand of Ezekiel."

Luis grabbed the box from the altar and smashed it into the sneering face.

Blood spurted from the monk's mouth as he fell sideways

to the ground, coughing, moaning. A spasm of pain shot up Luis's arm, a righteous punishment for his failure.

He leaned over the bleeding man, the box held high as a weapon. "Tell me where it is, and you will join me in glory."

The monk spat blood in Luis's face. "Never. I curse you and your crippled family as the Brotherhood has cursed all those who came before you."

Luis hammered the box down, battering the grinning face until all that was left was a bloody maw. His pants of exertion echoed around the bone chamber as the dead bore witness to the sacrifice.

After a last bubbling breath, the monk exhaled a final sigh.

Luis stood over the corpse, breathing heavily, the box in his hand covered in blood. His limbs ached, and he could feel the crack of his injuries hardening already. But it was worth it.

Julio put his hand out, pointed at the box. "What's that?"

Luis looked down. Blood had soaked into the joins of the tiny bones forming what looked like a map. He bent and dipped it into more of the monk's blood, using the life force to outline the path ahead.

Luis smiled. Of course, the Hand of Ezekiel would not be held in one place. But the Lord rewarded the faithful, and he had passed the first test.

He looked down at the dead body. "Get rid of that. Mark it and leave it somewhere public as a warning to those who might come after us. The Brotherhood of the Breath is broken but not finished yet."

Luis turned and walked back through the chamber. A shaft of sunlight broke through the clouds lighting the way ahead as he climbed out of the tomb into a new day, the bloody box of bone clutched tightly to his chest.

CHAPTER 2

New Orleans, USA.

AS THE TAXI PULLED up to the gates of the cemetery, Jake could see agent Naomi Locasto waiting outside in the shade of a turreted, brick building topped with the sculpture of a praying angel. Above her stretched an arch with decorative scrolls and the name of the place in filigree script – Saint Roch's, Campo Santo.

The area was cordoned off with yellow police tape, and a few officers walked the perimeter. Naomi stood apart from them wearing a cream linen suit that set off her dark skin. Somehow, she managed to look cool and serene even though the sun baked down and it was already sweltering hot. Naomi was truly a modern American citizen, her family a blend of African-American, Native American, and Eastern European immigrants. Proud of her heritage, she was a linguist, one of the finest they had working at ARKANE, and Jake wondered why she had chosen to work on this case – and why she had asked him to join her once more.

The Arcane Religious Knowledge And Numinous Experience (ARKANE) Institute investigated supernatural mysteries around the world, working in a realm beyond law enforcement, where the line between reality and the supernatural blurred. The last time they had worked together in New York, Naomi had killed her first man as they had fought to keep the blood of an angel from those who sought to use its power for evil. Jake wondered whether that death still haunted her, even as the shades of all those he had left behind still wandered his nightmares. By day, he could deny their power, but by night, their echoes remained.

Some of the things he had seen remained seared into his memory, but Jake couldn't step away, aware of what still lay out there threatening humanity. He was wary of this mission, unsure of what was to come, and if he was really honest, he was worried. His usual partner, Morgan Sierra, wasn't here with him and he wondered whether she would ever be again.

Jake paid the taxi driver and stepped out of the car with a sigh of relief. It was good to stretch his legs after the long flight from London. The heat hit him like a blast from an oven, and he felt a trickle of sweat down his spine under his white linen shirt. The light-headedness of jet lag swirled in his brain, but he pushed it aside, sharpening his focus as he strode over to Naomi in the shade.

"Welcome back, Jake. It's good to see you." Naomi smiled and leaned up to kiss him on the cheek. He held her briefly, her skin cool under his touch. They had been through a great deal together, although she still didn't know what he had seen under New York that final day. Perhaps he hadn't even seen it himself.

"It's good to be back." He smiled, the corkscrew scar above his left eye twisting up to his hairline. "I've never been to New Orleans, so I hope we get a chance to have a look around."

"This city will get under your skin, I promise. No one forgets The Big Easy. But first, I hope you can help with this case."

Naomi pointed up the wide path toward the chapel, and they walked together along the gravel, footsteps crunching, as they passed stone tombs ranged either side. Bright purple bougainvillea curled around the graves, scarlet hibiscus flowers blooming at the edges while the scent of waxy frangipani filled the air.

"Why are you working this case?" Jake asked. "I thought you preferred to be based in the New York office."

Naomi paused. She looked up at him, and Jake saw hesitation in her dark eyes. "It feels strange to say it out loud, but I think you'll understand." She took a deep breath. "I got bored."

Jake laughed. "Oh yeah, I know exactly what you mean. I go stir crazy if I'm not out on a mission. Director Marietti has given up trying to make me do office-work."

Naomi smiled, encouraged by his understanding. "I was lost before in all the books and relics and sacred objects and symbols and languages and, oh, so much paperwork. I could delve into a manuscript for days without thinking of the people behind the mystery. Those who died in the search for it. Or those lost because we didn't find it in time."

She pointed out the graves around them, some with colorful flower wreaths, others hung with plastic beads. "Besides, I know this place, these people. When the body was found, and ARKANE notified, I volunteered for the case. With my heritage, I'm a good match for this area. Saint Roch has always been racially mixed, home to one of the largest populations of free people of color since before the Civil War." She looked up at Jake. "But I don't think this is just a simple murder. I wouldn't have called you all the way over here otherwise."

They walked on to the chapel. It was simple compared to many Catholic churches, a cream facade with gold-painted trim and a tall arched window stretching up to a cross silhouetted against the bright, blue sky. A plaque dedicating the shrine to Saint Roch was carved above the door:

To the patron saint of miraculous cures,
in fulfillment of a sacred vow.

Jake glanced up at it as Naomi explained.

"There was a yellow fever epidemic here in 1867. A German priest, Reverend Thevis, prayed to Saint Roch, a fourteenth-century saint who cured plague victims in Italy. Thevis promised to build a shrine if no one in the parish died of it."

Jake grinned. "Let me guess. No one did."

"Exactly. So this place was built, and people still pray for healing here today – in a slightly macabre way."

They entered carefully, their footsteps echoing in the sanctuary as they walked down the aisle. Jake took a breath, the cool atmosphere refreshing after being outside. The air reeked of disinfectant but underneath, Jake could smell blood. Something shocking had torn the peace from this place. It was a sanctuary no longer.

The church was simple. Wooden pews lined up to face an altar flanked by paintings of the saint's life and a figurine of Saint Roch himself, a wide hat shading his eyes and a staff in his hand to guide the faithful onward. By his feet, a little dog looked up with soulful eyes, a piece of bread in its mouth.

"It's said that the dog saved his life," Naomi explained. "Roch nursed many plague victims, but eventually fell sick himself, and his dog brought him bread in the darkest moments."

Jake raised an eyebrow. "Everyone loves a happy dog story, right?"

Naomi laughed, the sound echoing in the space, a moment of levity before she glanced over to another door. "The body was found in there."

Jake walked over, opened the door and looked around at the strange scene. The room was filled with life-sized limbs, representations of the body parts that supplicants needed healing. There were plaster casts of feet in different sizes and shades, some flaking in the heat. Several legs were propped against the wall next to metal braces and crutches. Other objects cluttered every possible space on the shelves and window ledges – hearts, praying hands, crucifixes, coins, statues of saints and toys. A box with a pair of fake eyeballs sat on a shelf. At least Jake assumed they were fake.

The smell of blood was stronger in here. Flies buzzed as they thudded against the windows trying to escape. Nothing left to feed on now.

A sprayed outline of a body lay on the floor and within it, darker stains of blood that couldn't be scrubbed clean. Jake hunkered down next to it.

"The police took the body already?"

"They had to move it. The heat, you know." Naomi shrugged. "It's in the morgue." She handed Jake her smart phone. "These are the crime scene photos."

Jake scrolled through the pictures, noting the position of the dead man in the orientation of the room. His face had been beaten to a pulp, his body broken and bruised. There were occult markings carved into his skin, bloody lines forming distinct geometric patterns, crosses, stars and hearts. Jake noted the monk's robes, the emaciated body. This man didn't care much for his corporeal life, but clearly, faith sustained him.

"Do you know who he was?"

Naomi shook her head. "No trace of him so far. No prints. No dental records. We're searching through European databases as well."

"So apart from the fact that this guy was a monk, why is this an ARKANE case?"

"The occult markings, for a start." Naomi scrolled through the photos, zooming in to show the markings more clearly. "Some of these are *veve*, religious symbols of voodoo *loa*, or spirits. This is Baron Samedi's. This one for Maman

Brigitte. They were done post-mortem, so they didn't bleed much. That's why the lines are so clear."

Jake shrugged. "We're in New Orleans. Surely this kind of thing is pretty normal?"

"You've been watching too many zombie movies." Naomi pointed back to the pictures. "But that's not all. Check out his tattoo."

Jake scrolled further to a shot of the man's neck: a stylized tattoo of wind swirling around a cross of bone.

"It's certainly not a *veve*," Naomi said. "And it's not from a known gang. That's why we're here. The city is wary of religious killings, and with this political environment, they want to rule out extremism on any side."

Jake looked at the tattoo. If Morgan were here, she would probably know what it represented. But for now, he could always rely on Martin Klein back at ARKANE HQ in London. "I'll get Spooky on it. If there's something to be found, he'll find it."

Jake forwarded the photos onto Martin, knowing it wouldn't be long before they had a response. He looked at Naomi, eyebrows raised.

"It still doesn't explain why you consider this an ARKANE case. One body in a church with a symbol we'll probably trace within the hour?"

Naomi tilted her head to one side, her eyes twinkling with mischief. "I wanted you to see this place first – but wait until you see the hidden bone chamber discovered under the oldest cemetery in New Orleans."

Jake's eyes widened. "Now that sounds like my type of place."

* * *

ARKANE Headquarters, London, England.

Martin Klein examined the photo Jake had sent over. The straight bold lines of the bony cross. The curling wind giving it a sense of movement. He pushed his glasses up his nose, stretched his fingers out and delved into the world he loved best. The world of code and knowledge beyond the realms of the human brain. From this tiny office in the underground labyrinth hidden beneath Trafalgar Square, he could access a digital powerhouse.

Having recruited Martin from Cambridge University with a Doctorate in Computer Science and Archaeology, ARKANE Director Marietti had charged him with making sense of the chaos of data about religion and the supernatural. Over the years, Martin had raided archives from museums, libraries, private collections and secret societies around the world. An unseen relic hunter, leaving no trace of his digital fingerprints. It was spooky how fast he could find information, hence the nickname that Jake had given him, and that Martin not-so-secretly loved. But he could only steal what was available in bits and bytes, and so much of human knowledge lay in physical objects and hand-written scrolls stored in dusty libraries or carved into the walls of hidden tombs.

The everlasting search for knowledge drove ARKANE agents out into the field, solving mysteries, for sure, but also bringing back occult talismans, ancient manuscripts and objects of power for further study. Martin thought of the vault that lay beneath him, the security fully updated since the bombing that led them on a mission to India not so long ago. It was full of such artifacts gathered at great cost.

But the world was changing.

The digitalization of the Vatican Archives was a godsend to a white-hat hacker, as Martin considered himself. The project had begun in 2014 with the aim of putting the vast collection of Vatican Library manuscripts online for anyone to read. The team had started out with obvious texts of no significance – Renaissance Bibles, illustrated manuscripts, classical Greek and Latin works, papal bulls and ecclesiastical letters. But most of those working on the digitalization could not read what they scanned and photographed. As they accelerated the program, other texts began to slip through, perhaps by accident, perhaps by design. Valuable manuscripts with secrets that those with the right knowledge could access.

Martin had found some real gems while sifting through the millions of pages with his custom algorithm. He made sure to change the metadata afterwards so no one would know of his incursions – and it was doubtful that people would ever find the texts again in the mass of data.

The Vatican Library was one of the grandest collections in the world, but it was also one of the most useless because no human could possibly encompass the breadth of what lay inside. No single mind could process what lay inside the secret archives, or even the more accessible ones. Handwritten indexes had been copied from one to another as pages crumbled to dust. All it took was for one scribe to make a mistake on where a document was, or a deliberate miscopying designed to hide a secret in plain sight. A scholar might spend years applying for access and finally make it to Rome, only to never find what he searched for. But with digitalization, it might be possible to fathom what truly lay within those hallowed halls.

Martin aimed to collect the sum of all human knowledge in the ARKANE databases, his job title as Librarian an understatement for his life's work. An accumulation of every form of arcane and hidden knowledge the world had, from all cultures. With every year that passed, he gained access to more, and with the increasing possibilities of machine learning, he was able to delve deeper, finding links between disparate histories, surprising connections that explained ancient mysteries.

Once the original digitalization process had demonstrated its value, the Vatican had in recent months embraced new technologies with a project named *In Codice Ratio*, which used a combination of optical character recognition with artificial intelligence to search neglected texts going back to the eighth century. The aim was to take the fifty-three miles of corridors stacked with crumbling manuscripts and turn it into searchable text that could be used in a twenty-first-century Catholic faith.

It was in this maelstrom of knowledge that Martin finally found the symbol of wind swirling around a cross of bone. It was buried deep in the archives of the Spanish Inquisition, surrounded by dire warnings of what had been discovered in a bloody dungeon almost three hundred years ago. As Martin read the translation, his frown deepened, his eyes darkening in horror.

CHAPTER 3

Museo del Prado, Madrid, Spain.

AN ARMY OF SKELETONS overran the last of the living. They slaughtered the remnant of humanity with scythes and swords, drowning them, hanging them, carving them up. Two bony warriors rang a huge bell, tolling the death knell of the world as a haze of smoke burned across the ravaged, blackened land.

Morgan Sierra stared into Bruegel's *Triumph of Death*, wondering at how the Dutch painter had managed to capture his apocalyptic nightmare onto such a large canvas. How could he bear to turn his imagination into reality when it meant facing the horror anew every day, preserving it for all to behold. Morgan didn't think she could face her own nightmares like this. She had seen demons emerge from the Gates of Hell, the scar on her side throbbed from the fight in the bone church of Sedlec, and the burns on her legs sustained in the battle with the great serpent ached. And her mind ... well, her mind was definitely still on edge.

Tourists stood around her, listening to a museum guide explain the symbolism of Bruegel's sixteenth-century work. The skeletons were just a metaphor to show how death came to kings and paupers alike. But when Morgan looked at images like this, or at the Hieronymus Bosch nightmares in the room beyond, she knew that aspects of them were true. She half-expected the skeletons to emerge from the painting, swords raised high to slaughter those around her. Perhaps she was losing her ability to tell the difference between reality and fantasy.

Her mentor, Father Ben Costanza, had known how to balance the mundane routine of daily life with supernatural experience. He had been a man of faith, able to hold both realities in his mind, even as most people walked the earth with no clue as to the battle that waged in other realms. Tears welled up as Morgan thought of Ben and how she would never be able to ask his advice again.

A familiar voice broke into her thoughts. "There you are!"

Morgan turned from the painting to be enveloped in an expansive hug, the scent of wildflowers filling her senses as she embraced her dear friend, Dinah Mizrahi. Dinah was a clinical psychologist, Director of the Ezra Institute based in Israel. She specialized in those with Jerusalem Syndrome, who believed themselves to be prophets or other biblical figures. The pale horse of the apocalypse had shadowed Morgan and Dinah's steps when they had worked together once before – and it had been some time since they had caught up. When Dinah mentioned speaking at a conference in Madrid, Morgan had jumped on a plane to join her, glad of the chance to escape for a few days.

Dinah tilted her head to one side as she looked over at the painting. "That looks like your kind of fun." She laughed and took Morgan's hand. "Yalla, habibi. Let's go get a drink and some tapas."

They jumped in a cab and headed to one of the squares in the heart of La Latina, the oldest part of the city where tapas bars bumped up against ancient architecture and medieval streets. They found a table outside in a lively square tucked behind Iglesia de San Andrés Apóstol. Dinah called for wine and a selection of small plates – artichokes, asparagus and hard *manchego* cheese.

Morgan relaxed into the balmy evening as the familiar lilt of Spanish conversation rose around them. People catching up after work. Laughter. Normal life. No trace of skeletons with scythes. Morgan couldn't help smiling at herself. Clearly, she just needed a break.

Dinah held her glass up. "L'chaim. To life."

"To old friends and no drama," Morgan said. They clinked glasses and sipped at the full-bodied Ribera del Duero.

"So, what's been happening?" Dinah asked. "I heard you were in Jerusalem when that crazy serpent stuff was going on."

Morgan shook her head. "You wouldn't believe what went on under the Western Wall that day."

Dinah held her hand up. "And I don't want to know. It's probably classified anyway. But why aren't you out in the field now?"

Morgan took another sip of the wine, letting the heady scent of blackberries and spice relax her. "I walked out of ARKANE after the mission, and I don't know if I can go back. My friend ..." Her voice hitched as she bit back tears. "Well, he was more than a friend. More like a mentor. Father Ben Costanza."

Dinah nodded. "The monk who helped you so much at Oxford University."

"Yes. He died to protect an ancient seal. He tried to stop the End of Days – and even from beyond the grave, he saved my life and many others."

"And you feel guilty."

Morgan took a deep breath. "I feel like I'm surrounded by destruction. That I bring pain and death to my loved ones by being with ARKANE. Look at what happened with you and Lior in Jerusalem, and Faye and Gemma with the Pentecost stones. Even my father was killed for his beliefs as one of the Remnant."

"All of that's true, but you keep going back. Something is guiding you." Dinah put out a hand and took Morgan's. "For I know the plans I have for you, plans for welfare and not for evil, to give you a future and a hope."

"The book of Jeremiah," Morgan said, recognizing the sacred text. "But my faith remains on a knife-edge between science and the supernatural. I don't believe in the Judaism of my father, or the Christianity of my mother. I can't see the whole truth in either of them."

"But you've seen into the heart of evil, Morgan. I know that – and I know you haven't told me all that you've been through. Did Father Ben understand?"

Morgan nodded. "Yes, he did. His faith was strong and he died with the sure knowledge of where he would go next. Ben never shied away from facing evil."

She smiled as she remembered Ben's actions in India on the hunt for the weapon of Shiva Nataraja. Even as an old man, he had joined them to stop the Destroyer of Worlds.

Dinah swirled the red wine around her glass. "Exactly. He chose his life – as you have chosen yours. He wouldn't blame you for his death." She lifted her glass in a toast. "Father Ben."

Morgan raised her glass in turn. "To Father Ben."

Dinah leaned back in her chair. "So, what are you going to do next? Return to the university and your psychology practice?"

Morgan thought of her office tucked away near the Turf Tavern between Holywell Street and New College Lane in Oxford. When she left the Israeli Defense Force after the violent death of her husband, Elian, she had specialized in the psychology of religion. She had spent her first years at Oxford shuttling between the Theology faculty where divinity was uppermost, and the scientists of the psychology lab who had no patience for her religious leanings. Ben helped her marry the two as Morgan carved out a niche psychology practice helping cult survivors, but once she caught a glimpse of the world of ARKANE, she left all that behind.

After what she had seen beyond the veil of what most knew as reality, could she really go back to the mundane world of university politics and individual therapy?

She shook her head. "I don't know. There's still a place for me, but increasingly, it doesn't feel like home. Even my cat prefers the sitter these days."

"Adventure has its pros and cons." Dinah topped up her wine glass. "And what about your old partner, Jake Timber, wasn't it? Hot South African, I seem to remember." She gave a cheeky smile. "How's he doing without you?"

Morgan thought of Jake – his easy grin that twisted the corkscrew scar at his temple. His ferocity in battle and his unspoken tenderness.

Perhaps it was all about Jake. Perhaps she couldn't bear the thought of losing him as she had lost so many others. But had she lost him anyway by leaving ARKANE? He was in America now, on a mission with another agent – another partner. Did he even think of her?

* * *

St Louis Cemetery No. 1, New Orleans, USA.

This was more like it, Jake thought, as he followed Naomi through a narrow walkway between tightly packed vaults. New Orleans conjured many images in the minds of those who hadn't visited – jazz, Mardi Gras, floods – and of course, the graveyards, cities of the dead that remained at the heart of the old town.

A few palm trees grew, casting shade across the tombs but mostly the sun burned down from above onto stony ground. The majority of vaults were functional, rectangular, some with stone cladding crumbling away to reveal brick beneath, some fenced with spikes on top to keep people out – or perhaps to keep the dead in. Others had filigree crosses or statues of angels. Most were in a state of disrepair, but some were pristine, a beacon of white marble against the grey stone of old tombs. Fresh flowers adorned one grave carved with the names of a prominent family, whose most recent burial was just a year ago.

Jake thought of his own family, buried together as they had died, hacked to death in a raid gone wrong. He hadn't visited their grave in so long, preferring to stay away from South Africa and the memories he kept locked there. Back-to-back ARKANE missions meant that he never had time to think much about his own past – and that was fine. The living were his priority.

Naomi stopped in front of one tomb covered in hand-drawn 'X's with offerings of trinkets and plastic flowers lying in front.

"This is said to be the tomb of Marie Laveau, known as the Voodoo Queen."

"In a Catholic cemetery?"

"You'd be surprised how much of voodoo is related to Catholicism."

Naomi pointed at another tomb, an ostentatious white pyramid with the Latin inscription, *Omnia Ab Uno*, Everything From One. "That's the actor, Nicolas Cage's tomb, bought for when he dies."

"Put the bunny back in the box," Jake drawled in a terrible imitation of a southern accent.

Naomi looked confused.

Jake shrugged, a wry smile on his face. "*Con Air*. One of my favorite Cage movies."

"Must have been before my time," Naomi said, making Jake feel desperately old. "The collapse is at the back of the cemetery. This way."

They rounded the corner of a tomb to find a gaping hole with a mound of broken rock that led down into darkness surrounded by warning signs and safety rope.

"This is why the police called ARKANE," Naomi explained. "Traces of blood from the ground down there matched the body at Saint Roch. The monk was killed here, and then his body dumped – perhaps as a warning."

Naomi walked toward the hole, her footsteps sounding suddenly loud in the deserted cemetery.

Except it wasn't deserted.

Jake sensed something more here than the dust and ashes of the long-dead. The hairs on the back of his neck prickled, his jaw tightened, and his skin tingled even though the sun still beat down with intensity. In his years with ARKANE, he'd become attuned to energy beyond the visible.

Usually, he felt at peace in cemeteries, an acceptance of the passage of life that ended in eternal rest after a lifetime of struggle. But here, there was a twisting sensation, like the earth had been wrung out. The suffering and violent death of so many had trickled into the ground, filtering down to something beneath, festering in the dark. Now it had been disgorged.

Naomi turned around. "You coming?"

Jake followed and together they clambered down into the chamber.

Industrial standing lights lit up the scene below, reflecting off a ceiling of skulls, glancing off piles of bone, glinting from a sword held by a skeleton lying in battle pose. But what did it protect?

Jake caught his breath as the place brought back a memory of the battle with the demon in the bone church of Sedlec. He was a long way from the Czech Republic now, but that day, Morgan had saved his life. He looked over at Naomi as she gazed up at the walls. She was a good agent but new to the game, and he missed his partner. This trip was already turning into more than he had expected.

"How did they not know about this place before?" Jake asked.

Naomi walked toward the altar, carefully picking her way through the prone skeletons. "The surveyors swear it wasn't here. It just appeared somehow."

"Or it was built recently." But Jake's cynicism faded as he bent to the nearest skeleton, its skull coated in the patina of time. This was no modern re-creation of an ossuary. This had been constructed many years ago with the bones of slaves, the bones of the plague dead, the bones of those who went to death willingly – and those who resisted the darkness as it came for them.

Jake thought back to the chamber under New York City, a place shown on no map, with no way to find it again. A place somehow separate in time. He knew there were pockets in the world where energy warped and hidden things waited for the right time to emerge. So, what had emerged here?

"Look at this." Naomi pointed to the top of the altar. "There's a dust mark, an outline of a box that's been removed."

Jake came to stand next to her. "But who took it, and why?"

His phone rang, the tone a sudden intrusion.

Jake glanced at the screen. Martin Klein from ARKANE HQ. The connection was weak, so he walked back toward the opening so they could hear each other clearly.

"Hey, Spooky, what did you find?"

"Jake, this is much bigger than one murder. The symbol belongs to the Brotherhood of the Breath, a shadow organization that has protected a sacred relic for hundreds of years."

Jake looked around the chamber of bones. "What kind of relic? We have a few choices right here."

"The Brotherhood protect the Hand of Ezekiel, said to be able to raise the dead."

CHAPTER 4

"The Hand of Ezekiel?" Jake frowned. "Sounds like some kind of freaky mummified body part."

Naomi came to stand next to him, and he put the phone on speaker so she could hear Martin.

"It's unclear exactly what it is from the records but it's definitely in five pieces, and it refers to the book of Ezekiel, chapter 37, in verses known as the Valley of Dry Bones. The breath of God is summoned, and enters a vast army of the dead, bringing them back to life."

Jake shrugged. "I'm not an expert on biblical texts, but it sounds like a zombie story. A load of dead people coming back to life is pretty weird."

"Not so weird," Naomi said. "It's a metaphor for resurrection and new life."

A beat of silence.

"But what if it's not a metaphor," Martin said quietly. "What if it's actually real? After all, there are resurrection stories in many ancient religions, and zombies are accepted as a part of specific voodoo rituals."

Naomi looked puzzled. "I know Catholicism and voodoo have close ties, but what could possibly link a religious relic with zombies?"

"The history of Europe, Africa and the New World are

entwined with the blood and suffering of millions," Martin explained. "The Spanish acquired the Portuguese territories of Africa at the Treaty of El Pardo in 1778, but they were exploring territory there well before that. Even now, Spanish is the national language of Equatorial Guinea."

Naomi gasped at the name. "According to voodoo teaching, the entrance to the underworld can be found through seven gates scattered through the French Quarter here in New Orleans. The souls of the dead must pass through Guinee, a dark place presided over by the *loa*, Baron Samedi. The location of the Gates of Guinee is a closely held secret, and if they are opened in the incorrect way, evil spirits emerge to terrorize the living."

Jake frowned. "So that links the Spanish Empire with Guinea in Africa, and the slave trade brought West Africans to New Orleans along with voodoo –"

"– And perhaps pieces of the relic too," Martin interrupted, his enthusiasm spilling over. "It would make sense if it were scattered across the New World and the Old."

"Nothing about this makes sense," Jake said. "But that's not unusual for an ARKANE mission."

"Start with the links to the Spanish Inquisition in New Orleans," Martin said. "I'll keep digging and see what else I can discover here."

They ended the call. Jake looked at Naomi. "So where do we start?"

"I know just the place."

* * *

Charity Hospital, New Orleans, USA.

Luis Rey had a townhouse in the historic Faubourg Marigny district – a tiny part of his vast family fortune that had accumulated since the days of the Spanish Empire – but the abandoned Charity Hospital was where he did his real work. When Hurricane Katrina had ripped New Orleans apart, many buildings had never been reclaimed. They lay empty in ruins, fenced off, forgotten except by those who wished to keep their activities away from prying eyes.

Luis shuffled through the abandoned corridors of the hospital carrying the box of bone, his nose wrinkling at the smell of decay. The faded flood tide marks could still be seen on the walls, brown smudges from stagnant water, a toxic soup of human waste, chemical spills, agricultural runoff, and the rotting remains of those who had perished in the floods. All part of a facade now. There were other entrances in nondescript buildings that came in through underground tunnels, but Luis preferred this one. The drip of water, the smell of death, all kept him focused on his goal.

Everything dies. Everything turns to dust. But what if death itself could be beaten?

There was a kind of beauty in the decaying building, but its primary purpose was to keep people out. Homeless vagrants who had wandered in over the years looking for a place to sleep had become part of the experiments. Likewise the urban explorers, the ruin hunters, whose disappearance had been counted by local police as a natural end to the risks they took willingly in the shadows.

Deep inside the shell of the building, hidden within layers of security, Luis had constructed a research lab and private clinic, funded by his fortune and billionaire backers from Silicon Valley as well as clandestine departments of the military. All chased immortality, and now he was a step closer.

Money kept the law away, and money brought scientists to his door. Those who had been discredited for research on the edge of ethics. Those from foreign powers who wanted a new start in America and who would do anything for a green card. Those who were willing to take a devil's bargain and search for a way to resurrect the dead, to turn dry bones and decaying flesh into living beings again. Generations of Reys had trusted in God to reveal the final resting place of the Hand of Ezekiel, but Luis wasn't willing to wait any longer. He clutched the box of bone to his chest. Perhaps this would provide the missing piece.

He turned into one of the disused treatment rooms to the side of the main entrance hall. Broken furniture and used syringes lay strewn about the floor. Not a place to linger. Luis walked a slow path through the debris, stepping over the discarded needles which were all tagged for security, setting off alarms if they were moved. At the back of the office, he opened a plain cupboard door and stepped inside, closing it behind him.

A metallic click. A buzzing sound as lasers scanned him for biomarkers.

The back of the cupboard swung open, and Luis stepped into his true home. The high-tech lab was quiet, just the faint hum of medical equipment and the low discussion of hard-working scientists. It smelled of antiseptic, a stringent note that matched the gleaming surfaces around him.

Several glass-walled rooms circled the entranceway, and Luis glanced in at the work in progress as he walked by. In one, a body in an advanced state of putrefaction lay on a gurney while a scientist in a white hazmat suit sliced into its flesh. In another, a young Latino man fought his captors only to be subdued by a needle, before he was strapped down and a mask placed over his face. Luis was glad to see a live one – fresh dead were ideal to experiment on and it was best to keep them sedated until his team had a new batch of powder to test.

Every subject was another step toward the ultimate goal. Each gave their lives to the worthy cause of conquering death – and if they didn't choose the path willingly, well,

God would know His own at the end of it all.

Luis walked to the glass window and tapped lightly upon it. One of the scientists looked up and nodded. She placed the syringe down and stepped outside the room, peeling her hazmat suit away from her face.

With her flawless tawny skin and sapphire eyes, the result of her mixed Creole heritage, Lashonda Milton could have won Miss Louisiana if she had been so inclined. She wore brilliant blue beads wound through her hair, but mostly, she wore her beauty like the outer skin it really was, preferring to pursue the fascinations of the mind. Lashonda had tested at genius level throughout high school, but she had been denied her rightful place at Ivy League universities, judged for her looks, her poverty, and her name. But their loss was Luis's gain, and Lashonda had joined his team as a young scientist with ambition, a keen desire to learn, and no ethical issues with his experiments.

She managed to compartmentalize her life between the science of her job, the Catholic faith of her Sunday mornings, and the voodoo celebrations of St John's Day. Luis had an inkling of the nights she spent in the bayou at secret gatherings of the faithful, but he understood the different facets of her nature. After all, Creole was about the mix of cultures. These days, she was his most trusted scientist, one of the few who understood the scope of what Luis wanted to achieve, working with him to shift the line between life and death.

Lashonda ran a hand through her dark curls and gestured at the prone Latino man. "That one is strong. He'll be a good subject for the next batch."

Luis held out the box of bone. "I need you to analyze this before you continue with anything else."

Lashonda grabbed a new pair of sterile gloves and snapped them on before taking it from him. Her eyes widened. "Is this –?"

Luis nodded. "I think so. Finally. But I need to know the age of the bones and their composition. It could be a hoax."

Lashonda lifted the box and looked at the intricate bony design, noting the fresh crimson inlay. "You want the blood analyzed as well as the bones?"

Luis shook his head. "No need. I know where that's from."

"I'll get on it right now."

Lashonda turned away, walking with measured steps to her personal lab while Luis entered a small elevator and ascended to his private office. He put his hand on the door handle and waited a second for the biometric scan to complete before it clicked open.

This was his private domain, the heart of the medical lab and where he kept the records of previous experiments under lock and key. Racks of files crowded one half of the room, each containing evidence of a tiny step toward life after death. The rats they had brought back from the dead, shaking, blistering, but alive for seconds nonetheless. The putrefied bodies they had reverted back to a semblance of living flesh. A catalogue of trial and error.

But there was still space reserved on the racks for the next wave of research, the final step toward resurrection. Luis rubbed his aching limbs, aware of the ossification that advanced every day. They were so close. He just needed the final piece – the promise of the Hand of Ezekiel.

He crossed to the far wall of his office. It was nothing special to look at, merely another white wall with a painting of the Risen Christ upon it. Luis removed the canvas, undid a simple catch and pulled open the shutters revealed beneath. Behind them lay his family altar – a simple wooden table handed down through generations, upon which lay a Bible and a Book of Days, a journal that held the writings of the monk whose secret lay beneath this modern quest.

The legend of the Hand of Ezekiel had been passed down through the Rey family line, along with the disease that ossified them slowly, turning each to bone. It was said that the secret to raising the dead had been found in West Africa, in what is known today as Equatorial Guinea. A monk, Miguel Rey, had witnessed a whole village rise from a mass grave at the hands of a witch doctor. Whereas many would have dismissed such events as demonic, a trick of the darkness that held the continent in its embrace, the monk remembered the prophecy of Ezekiel's Valley of Dry Bones. He saw a power that could be used by the Spanish Empire to renew its forces, overstretched as they were across the New World and in danger of losing what had been hard won with blood and steel.

The monk risked his life to steal the witch doctor's secret and took it back to Spain, a gift for the Catholic Church. But he was betrayed, the Hand of Ezekiel stolen. In the bloody chambers of the Spanish Inquisition, Miguel's body was torn apart while he confessed to sinister sacrificial rites, summoning the devil, anything to stop the pain. The Hand disappeared into the vaults of the Inquisitors, protected as a dark secret never to be spoken of again.

Condemned to burn at the stake, his brother, the first Luis Rey of the line, visited the monk in the dungeons of Toledo and Miguel recounted the whole story. As his dying screams echoed around the square the next day, as the fire turned him to ash, his brother vowed to avenge him and show the Catholic Church that resurrection was not just a gift of God, but could be summoned by the hand of man.

Thus began a quest across the generations as the Rey family sought to find the Hand of Ezekiel. Over the centuries, the Inquisition lost its power, going underground, taking its secrets into shadow. The Hand was thought lost, but the emergence of the Brotherhood of the Breath at the crypt meant that they were close at last.

A knock at the door interrupted his thoughts.

Luis turned and buzzed Lashonda in. She placed the box gently on his desk, her fingers lightly caressing the ridges on its surface.

"The bones are from the mid to late seventeenth century. Most are from children, a mix of Spanish and West African descent."

Luis let out a deep breath and leaned forward to look more closely. "It's real then."

Lashonda nodded. "But the box is empty. We still have to find the Hand."

Luis turned the box upside down, the crimson lines revealing a map of the ancient Spanish Empire. It stretched from West Africa to Spain, from the New World and into Asia, the outlines of nations intricately constructed from the shards of tiny bone. Five blood-red rubies shone under the light of the desk lamp, marking places where the Spanish had once reigned.

"But now we know where to start looking."

CHAPTER 5

Jackson Square, New Orleans, USA.

THE WAITER PUT DOWN a plate of what looked like powdered sugar. Naomi reached over and dug through to the fried pastry beneath, sending clouds of white over the marble tabletop.

"You can't come to New Orleans without trying *beignets* at Café du Monde." She took a bite and grinned. "Hmm, heart attack on a plate. You gotta try them."

The sweet baked smell made Jake's mouth water. He tucked in, and between them, they polished off a plateful along with cups of *café au lait*. "Not bad for a tourist trap."

Fueled up with sugar and caffeine, they walked across Decatur Street to Jackson Square, past rows of tourists queuing for the horse and carriage tours, and on toward the street artists gathered in the shade of live oak and magnolia trees.

An ornate metal fence surrounded the historic park in the French Quarter, every inch hung with hand-made art. Bright paintings of sugar skulls next to black and white line drawings of jazz icons, watercolors of the city streets next to abstract representations of the Deep South. Highly skilled painters sat next to hawkers selling cheap souvenirs.

Tarot card readers rested under striped umbrellas, each a way to see into the world beyond, while above them, multi-colored Mardi Gras beads hung from the trees, a reminder of worldly pleasure. The sound of music filled the air – the deep sonorous notes of a saxophone, the bright notes of a fiddle, then around the corner, a girl with a guitar, her voice an offering to whatever spirits walked the streets today in human guise.

Jake and Naomi ambled through the square, weaving through the tourist crowd, looking up at St Louis Cathedral before them. Its facade was the color of ivory dulled by the passage of time, with three spires covered in black tiles rising above, a clock face on the middle one. The two side turrets had patriarchal crosses mounted high up, with an extra line above the central crossbar.

"It was a simple wooden structure when the settlers built the first church here in 1718," Naomi explained. "They constructed a more robust brick and timber church later but it burned down in the Great Fire of 1788, and this version was constructed in 1850."

Jake weighed it against the great cathedrals of Europe and found it wanting. St Louis was the oldest cathedral in the United States, the seat of the Roman Catholic Archdiocese of New Orleans, but it was tiny in comparison to the impressive edifices of Catholic Spain and France.

"How does it link to the Inquisition?"

Naomi pointed to the Cabildo on the left of the cathedral. "That used to be the Spanish colonial city hall. There's a painting inside that you need to see."

They walked over and entered through a grand doorway, the cool semi-darkness a relief after the close heat outside. The interior reminded Jake of a European stately home, faded grandeur, old paintings of forgotten faces ignored by tourists on smart phones looking for something more dramatic to photograph. There was a sense of disrepair, a quiet, dusty memory in comparison to the vibrant life played out on the streets of Jackson Square outside.

Naomi walked ahead, her heels clicking on the stone floor until she stopped in front of a huge painting. "Here he is. Supreme Officer of the Holy Inquisition of Cartagena in Louisiana."

The painting of Father Antonio de Sedella, known as Père Antoine, was as large as the wall. The friar stared out from the past, his dark eyes serious, with a prominent nose and generous lips. His tonsured hair was white and his beard hung down to the front of his black habit. The stone arch of the cathedral framed his figure as he stretched out a hand toward a book on a green table. A russet chair and scarlet curtain completed the image, the colors echoing the bloody history of the church he served.

"Despite his austere gaze, Père Antoine was known to be kind to his parishioners, even the slaves." Naomi scanned the text next to the painting. "He was a Capuchin friar, originally from Malaga in the south of Spain. He arrived in New Orleans in 1774 as an official of the Inquisition and became pastor of St Louis. The Tribunal of the Inquisition wasn't active here, but he still had their jurisdiction."

Jake leaned toward the painting to look more closely at the table in front of the friar. "You'd expect him to be reading a Bible, but the book is too thin." The faint text on the spine was just legible. "It's Ezekiel. Strange. What else does the text say?"

Naomi paused. "Oh, that is weird. He baptized Marie Laveau and presided over her wedding in 1819."

"What's weird about that?"

Naomi turned to him, her eyes wide. "Marie Laveau, the Voodoo Queen, remember? We saw her grave in St Louis cemetery No. 1." She raised an eyebrow. "There's no way Père Antoine could have been ignorant of her practices. It's another link between voodoo and Catholicism."

Cases containing books and letters from the time surrounded the painting. Most were dull, ecclesiastical records but one in particular caught Jake's eye. A letter in looping, generous handwriting, the mark of an educated man.

"It says here that Père Antoine was blamed by some for the destruction of the city in the Great Fire of 1788. He refused to have the bells ring out in warning as it was Good Friday and as such was prohibited."

Naomi looked puzzled. "That doesn't make sense. Other records show he was often a rebel against the official religious law, acting in defense of his parishioners and for the greater good. What possible reason could he have for wanting to burn down the city?"

Jake raised an eyebrow. "Maybe there was something that could only be destroyed by fire, something he didn't want to be found." He turned and looked into the eyes of the friar, trying to figure out the man across the centuries. "What were you hiding?"

Naomi put a hand on Jake's arm. "He was buried in the cathedral, and it's said he haunts the place. Perhaps we should go look inside? See if we can find anything else that might help."

They walked out of the Cabildo and into the cathedral next door, entering behind a group of teenagers who chatted away in French while ignoring their local guide in front.

Inside the cathedral, Jake looked up at the vaulted nave, where paintings of saints looked down upon the faithful. Flags from different nations hung at the top of tall pillars above the pews. A restrained altar by Catholic standards sat below a massive painting of Louis IX, King of France, embarking on a crusade, a holy war to destroy the unbelievers. Jake shook his head and sighed. Humans didn't change. Always demonizing the Other, claiming truth as their own and killing those who stood against them.

He turned around slowly, letting the atmosphere of the

place sink in. It felt far more like a tourist location than a place of worship, the level of noise more suited to a theme park than a cathedral. It was warm, balmy even, a sensation he struggled to associate with the huge stone edifices of Europe that kept the faithful shivering on their knees. The believers here were comfortable, with no trace of hardship or suffering. Even the painted saints looked well fed, clothed in finery, their faces belonging to the wealthy patrons of European heritage, not the itinerant preachers of the early believers in the Middle East.

Jake looked over at Naomi as she examined the place, her darker skin unrepresented even though the city was filled with people of color whose faith sustained the church.

She turned at his gaze and pointed behind him. "At least they have a woman in here."

Jake spun around and looked up at a statue of Saint Jeanne d'Arc. She wore the armor of a French nobleman, a standard clutched in her hand as she stared toward the altar, a challenge in her eyes.

"They certainly like fire in this city," he said softly, ideas beginning to swirl in his mind as to what dark secrets lay beneath the veneer of this elegant house of prayer.

He noticed a Bible in a glass case at the foot of the plinth, a thick tome opened to an illustrated page. Jake stepped closer to see the text. Ezekiel chapter 37, the Valley of Dry Bones. Skeletal figures crawled from the earth around the edge of the page, blank eyes fixed on the prophet as he stretched out his hand to call the dead from the grave.

"It's a copy of the Bible of St Louis." Naomi read from the plaque next to it. "Illustrated between 1226 and 1234 in Paris, it's also known as the Toledo Bible. The original is in the Cathedral of Toledo in Spain." Her eyes darkened, a frown deepening between her brows. "The Catholic Church purged Toledo during the Reconquista. The streets ran with the blood of the Jews they slaughtered."

"A dark history, indeed. Perhaps they were hiding something there. These images don't look medieval, and look at that." Jake pointed to the stylized image of a cross surrounded by the wind in one corner of the page. "The mark of the Brotherhood of the Breath."

Naomi put her finger on the glass case, as if trying to touch the symbol through the barrier. "This is just a copy, perhaps there is something different in the original? But we can't go to Toledo, not now. We have too much to investigate here."

Jake took a deep breath. "I might know someone who can help us."

* * *

Madrid, Spain.

Morgan wandered through the streets of La Latina. She had dropped Dinah back to the hotel and then headed out again, restlessness keeping her from sleep. She walked alone, surrounded by the nightlife of the vibrant city. Her stride was that of a predator, not a victim, and as she pulled the night around her, she lost herself in tiny passageways, emerging into plazas dominated by the ever-present churches, the power of faith still pervasive even in modern Spain.

The smell of sweet *churros* hung in the air from the night market stalls as the sound of vendors hawking their wares filled the balmy night. The sound of music wafted from bars and Morgan glimpsed friends drinking together, and the dance of courtship between strangers that was obvious in any culture. Her scars throbbed, but the pain of her burned flesh helped her think, grounding her to the earth as she walked on.

Morgan glimpsed her own history in the features of those passing by. She had inherited the Sephardi Jewish looks of her Spanish father, Leon Sierra, murdered as one of the Remnant. He was buried in a Kabbalah cemetery in Safed in Israel, safe now from those she had pursued in vengeance through Moorish Spain not so long ago. She shivered as she remembered the Gates of Hell, but what she had seen that final night was the fuel that drove her now. She could not un-see the darkness that some would try to bring into the world, but her life had no meaning unless she tried to stop them.

Morgan brushed a dark curl back from her face, noting how much she fitted in here, easily passing as a *Madrileña*, a native of the city. Perhaps she should move over, leave the stifled sensibilities of Oxford for the laid-back freedom of Spain. She smiled to herself. Whenever she was restless, she thought about moving in the hope that it might help tame the wildness that lay within her. But moving only quietened it for a time, before something rose to drive her on to something new.

Would she ever find peace? Would there ever be a place that she could call home, somewhere to put down roots and build a life she could share with another?

Once she had thought it would be Israel, but when her husband Elian had died in a hail of bullets on the Golan Heights, she had left the country she had grown up in for a new life. Perhaps she had been running ever since.

The scream of a siren suddenly split the air.

People looked around with concern, bodies poised for flight. *Madrileños* still remembered the commuter train bombings of 2004, the threat of terrorism remaining in a country with so many from far corners of the earth. But the siren passed by and smiles returned, the life of the night market continuing. Another sip of wine. Another flirtatious smile. Another moment of life.

Morgan felt the vibration of her phone in her pocket and stopped in the entranceway of a church to pull it out.

Jake. Her heart beat a little faster as she saw his name.

There was a moment when she considered not answering it. Did she want whatever he offered?

Morgan looked around, recognizing the mundanity of life here, just as it was in every place she ran to. There was only one way to escape the turmoil inside her, to live a life of freedom. She had to embrace the chaos.

She answered the phone.

CHAPTER 6

MORGAN TOOK A DEEP breath as the line connected. "Hi, Jake."

"Sorry to call so late." His voice was hesitant. "I didn't know if you'd be awake."

"Madrid only wakes up around ten pm, so we're just getting started." Morgan could hear sounds of a saxophone and the chatter of a crowd at the other end of the line. "How's New Orleans?"

"You'd like it here."

"You'd like it here, too."

A beat of silence between them.

"Since you are there," Jake continued. "I wondered if perhaps you wouldn't mind jumping on a train to Toledo."

Morgan leaned back against the cool stone of the church behind her, the wall hard and unyielding, just like the faith it represented. "It's only an hour away. What do you need?"

"There's a Bible in the cathedral. We need to compare the original Ezekiel chapter 37 with the copy here in New Orleans."

Morgan took another deep breath. "I'll need special access. Permissions."

"I'll get Martin to meet you there tomorrow."

Morgan could hear the smile in Jake's voice and found herself grinning in return. "It will be good to see him."

* * *

Charity Hospital, New Orleans, USA.

Behind the labs and holding cells, beyond the reach of beeping monitors and the struggle to synthesize life, there was a private wing of the hospital, a series of luxury apartments for those guests who came to the clinic in secret. There was no illegality in what they did here, but sometimes the line blurred between what was legal and what was ethical.

Luis walked down the long corridor past frosted glass doors, the sound of low voices inside. Clients paid handsomely for guaranteed privacy on top of the treatments they sought – a regimen that wound back the clock on their biological lifespan. Luis smiled to himself as he recalled the names of notable people inside, the millions that poured into his bank accounts daily.

A doctor walked down the corridor pushing a cart with a red box on top marked Blood Products in Transit. The doctor nodded respectfully at Luis and paused by one of the luxury suites, entering a code on the door before stepping inside.

The idea of taking blood from the young and injecting it into the old was first postulated by the natural philosopher Robert Boyle in the seventeenth century. Once considered ethically abhorrent and even vampiric, there were now Silicon Valley start-ups that provided the service from private blood banks. There were rumors of clandestine clinics in Latin America that offered blood from those too young to give consent, but here in New Orleans, Luis made sure they were legally above board. Many wanted to try the service and paid handsomely for it.

Life extension had become an obsession for those wealthy enough to satisfy every desire. As bio-technology leapt ahead, radical life extension was becoming a possibility, driven by Silicon Valley billionaires who were arrogant enough to want to beat death. Some researched backing up their consciousness onto quantum computers, others investigated using shell bodies, or clones; others still at regeneration at the cell level. These men, and they were mostly men, were not willing to fade away, to let death rob them of their power and make them equal to any pauper dying in the gutter.

Some questioned whether humans should tinker with lifespan and Luis had even watched a live stream of a debate at the Vatican on the ethics of life extension. One of the speakers argued that longevity had a Biblical basis: 'Methuselah lived 969 years according to Genesis chapter five. Death comes to us all, but it doesn't have to come in three score years and ten.'

There were ethical issues, of course, around sustainability of the planet with an undying population, but most acknowledged that life extension was a valid pursuit.

Unfortunately, it had a fatal flaw.

Accidents happened, and unless you spent your life cocooned in a padded cell, no one could stop death from arriving around a blind corner. When a billionaire's beloved son died in a car accident, the grieving father found his way to Luis's door.

The first Reys had sought the Hand of Ezekiel for religious purposes, but Luis had recognized its commercial potential. Bringing back the dead for some kind of divine army was unnecessary in a world of drones and cyber-terrorism. But bringing back the dead for those who could pay for it was an entirely different matter. The hunt for the relic suddenly had unlimited funding.

They had made little progress, but now the bone box and its map might change everything, and Luis could only hope they would find it in time. He had his own reasons to find what could turn dry bone into living flesh again. He walked on down the corridor, his footsteps quickening, each step matching a heartbeat toward the inevitable end.

Beyond the luxury apartments, Luis had his own private suite. He paused at the door and bent forward, leaning his forehead against the wall. The coolness soothed him for a moment as he struggled to turn his expression from concern to confidence. He breathed deeply and inhaled the floral scent that overlaid the antiseptic smell. The cloying fragrance reminded him of a funeral home, and he almost gagged at the thought that he might have to visit her in such a place. It wasn't right for someone so young.

He stood upright again, as upright as he could with his twisted spine, and plastered a smile on his face. He pressed the button by the automatic door and it swished to the side.

"Morning, sweetheart."

Elena Rey sat in the hospital bed, propped up by pillows. Her mahogany hair hung like a curtain around her face, her olive skin pale. A drip fed into her left arm and monitors surrounded her, leads attached to sensors on her skin, continually monitoring her condition. Her dark brown eyes opened and she smiled to see him.

"Morning, Papa."

Her voice was so weak, and her eyes betrayed a deep exhaustion. Luis wished he could take her out of here, back to the beaches of southern Spain where she could run and dance with other teenagers, in love with life. But instead, she was here, waiting to die. Luis knew she was ready to go – but he wasn't willing to give her up.

Elena was born thirteen years ago, the result of a casual relationship. Luis had never cared much for her mother, but when his little girl entered the world, he had fallen in love for the first and only time. His lawyers made sure he had full custody and his baby girl had everything.

But one day, his sweet Elena had fallen and bruised

herself. As the muscle ossified, the look in the doctor's eyes that day told him everything.

His own genetic code damned his daughter to an early death. Her variation of Fibrodysplasia ossificans progressiva was particularly aggressive and even stretching a muscle too much could cause acceleration of bone development. Elena's body was soon covered in the tumor-like lumps that characterized the disease, and she became bed-ridden before her tenth birthday.

Some in his family called it God's will. Some said it was unfortunate that the disease had developed so young, but he would have more children. There would be more Reys to carry on the family line.

But Luis would not let Elena go so easily. He worked with every specialist he could find in the world until they all said there was nothing left to do. That he should prepare for the end. So, Luis brought her to the lab, his determination renewed. He would find the Hand of Ezekiel, and it would bring life to the bones that crippled his beloved.

He picked up the tablet computer that monitored Elena's condition, tapped it to find the latest results and reviewed the most recent scans. The chart showed a marked increase in bone formation around Elena's ribcage. It wouldn't be long until the ossification process stopped her breathing altogether.

Luis kept his smile in place. "It's looking better, sweetheart, and I have some exciting new possibilities that are going to help you."

Elena looked up at him, deep purple shadows under her eyes. She spoke in a halting whisper. "It hurts, Papa. I'm so tired. Can't I just rest?"

Luis knew what she meant. They had talked about her end of life choices, and when she said enough was enough, he would respect her decision to sleep without pain. He would help her transition and make sure she didn't feel a thing except peace and love at the end.

But he couldn't let her go just yet.

Luis blinked back the tears that pricked at his eyes. He sat down on the side of her bed and gently took her hand in his.

"Of course, I want you to rest. But I need you to hang on. I really do have something that might change things. Will you give me a little more time?"

Elena looked up at him, devotion in her eyes. She sighed. "A little more time, Papa. But only a little."

Luis bent to kiss her forehead, hiding his tears as he placed his lips against her skin. She was soft and warm, still alive. At least for another day. He reached for the controller to the pain meds that dripped into her arm. He pressed one of the buttons, releasing a tiny dose.

"I'll let you sleep now."

Luis walked to the door, then turned back. Elena lay with her eyes closed, her skin as pale as a corpse, her petite frame already made of so much bone. It was a wonder she still breathed.

There wasn't much time left.

He needed the Hand of Ezekiel to turn her dry bones back to life again. Luis clenched his fists. Nothing would stop him finding that relic.

Back in his office, he picked up the bone box and looked at the intricately placed rubies. He compared the positions to a map of the Spanish Empire, then he called Julio.

"It's time. The first location is Toledo."

CHAPTER 7

Toledo, Spain.

MORGAN STEPPED OUT OF the taxi and looked out over the entire city on the other side of the valley. The clouds parted, and the sun shone down on the Alcazar dominating the skyline with its four turrets and thick walls. It overlooked closely packed houses below that ran all the way down to the waterline in a riot of terracotta roofs, grey stone and green trees.

Toledo was the perfect defendable city, built on a mountaintop, surrounded on three sides by the rush of the Tagus River. It was formidable indeed, and Morgan felt the chill of what it represented for her ancestors as she got back in the taxi and they headed in toward the city gates.

Although small in size, the ancient city of Toledo loomed large in history. Originally a Roman town, it became the capital of the Visigoth kingdom for centuries. Synods, church councils, had been held in Toledo for the first thousand years of Christianity, turning the city into a center of learning.

But when the Moors took the Iberian Peninsula in the early eighth century, Toledo entered a period of decline.

Re-taken by the Christian king, Alfonso VI of Castile, in 1085, its cultural center was revived and later, Toledo was the first concrete step in the Reconquista, as the Christian monarchs took Spain back from Muslim rule.

But the medieval years were hard for the Jews of Toledo. They were persecuted and killed, forced to convert, and in 1492, forced from their homes and driven into exile. When Toledo became home to the court of Charles V, the Holy Roman Emperor, it was known for embracing elements of the Jewish, Christian and Muslim faiths, but the Catholic Church still ruled here even now.

Morgan stepped out of the taxi at the city gates and walked into the pedestrianized streets. The main thoroughfare was a tourist trap with shops selling *jamon*, the ubiquitous cured ham of the region, bad replicas of Toledo steel swords and plastic Madonnas. It was disappointing, a medieval theme park with no sense of the history that Morgan had glimpsed from the outer city.

But then she turned a corner into a narrow alleyway that led into the oldest part of the city. Clouds gathered above, the sky darkened, and as it began to rain, the tourist crowds disappeared into coffee shops. Morgan walked alone at last, and a glimpse of the old city revealed itself in the stone walls that loomed high around her. A canopy of faded red cloth hung down from above with embroidered floral decoration, wreaths of flowers draped at intervals along it. A walkway for the faithful as they came to pray, leading to the cathedral gate.

Martin Klein stood at the entrance, bobbing up and down on the balls of his feet. His shock of rough-cut blonde hair spiked in different directions, his wire-rim glasses and eager gaze made him look like an escaped professor. Morgan smiled to see him. ARKANE's archivist was far more than his job title, and Martin had joined the team on a number of missions, although he still hadn't quite learned to navigate the real world as well as his virtual one.

"Morgan, so lovely to see you."

Martin bobbed toward her a little and then ducked away. She didn't try to hug him, respecting his need for physical distance, an integral part of his personality.

"I'm glad you're here, Martin. I'm still not really sure what Jake wants with this Toledo Bible."

"I don't think he knows either, but let's have a look. I arranged permission with the Librarian here. There should be someone to meet us by the choir and take us to the Bible."

They entered the door into the cathedral, walking into chilly darkness as they stepped over the threshold. It was freezing, and as Morgan looked up to the arched ceiling high above, she could see why.

The cathedral was massive, an enormous space. It was the very definition of the Gothic style, built in the thirteenth century and extended in the fifteenth, on the foundations of the Visigoth basilica. Stone pillars towered above, meeting in soaring arches. Stained glass windows let in a little light, but as the rain poured down outside, it sent the cathedral further into shadow. Morgan shivered. In some places of faith, she felt warmth and welcome, but here, she felt only numbing cold.

They explored inside, looking around at the five naves that covered a vast footprint over the heart of the ancient city, a determined effort to build over the former mosque and *sahn*, Islamic courtyard, from the reign of the Moors. Chapels dedicated to various saints lay between massive stone pillars and an ornate choir dominated the center of the cathedral. The atmosphere was somber, as faces of tortured saints gazed down on unhappy pilgrims.

They passed one chapel with a surprising mural above the altar – the siege and capture of Oran, a famous Spanish victory in North Africa against the Moors of Algiers. The glorification of war ever present in this house of God.

"They celebrate a Mozarabic rite here," Martin explained.

"An early liturgy that dates back to the Visigoths and used by Christians who lived under Muslim rule. Quite unusual."

They rounded the front of the main chapel. Morgan stepped past a gilded gate and up into the ornate choir, every inch of the stone carved with saints and prophets, every walnut-wood seat decorated with Christian images. At least that's what they looked like at first glance, but as Morgan examined them more closely, she noticed unusual figures within the carvings. A dragon eating its own tail in a figure-of-eight, the symbol of infinity. A misshapen man with a face in his chest, one of the fabled creatures who lived off the edge of maps in medieval times. A dragon fighting a man with the head of an elephant. It was a curious collection, and Morgan wondered what hidden meanings might be laid out in this place. At another time, she might have looked for them, but they were only here for the Bible today.

Morgan and Martin stood together next to the choir gate, looking around for anyone resembling a librarian. Tourists wandered past, phones raised high, taking pictures of the martyred saints around them.

Eventually, a monk with the face of a crumpled gargoyle approached them. He beckoned with one spindly finger.

"Come." He spun around and walked off.

Morgan raised an eyebrow at Martin. He shrugged, and they both followed like errant schoolchildren.

The taciturn monk led them through a tight corridor of towering stone, zigzagging around corners until they emerged into the cloisters, a covered walkway around a courtyard where geese waddled through a grove of orange trees. A surprising oasis in the heart of the freezing cathedral.

On one side of the quadrangle, a row of wooden doors led into rooms beyond. The monk pointed at the end one, nodding toward it.

Morgan and Martin walked over, pushed the door and

entered. Two doors led off either side of a stained glass window in the large room. Glass cabinets around the walls contained objects from the cathedral's history – ornate candelabra, panels of painted saints, ritual cups and liturgical texts. In one case, a series of Toledo steel knives lay nestled in black velvet. Morgan leaned over to look more closely at the swirling pattern on the blades.

"These are beautiful." She could almost feel the satisfying heft of the weight in her hand. A memory rose of training in the Negev desert with the Israeli Defense Force, learning how to wield a knife, how to defend with one. The sharp blade of memory cut through her as she recalled Elian's laughing face as they tussled in the dust in the days before everything changed.

"Toledo steel has been used in sword-making for almost two thousand years," Martin said, interrupting her thoughts. "The Roman legions used it from the time of Hannibal." He walked to the heavy wooden table in the middle of the room. "But this is what we really came for."

The Toledo Bible lay propped up on a wooden slatted base, two pairs of white gloves next to it. The monk stood by the door, watching while Morgan and Martin put the gloves on. He nodded once in satisfaction and went to sit under the orange trees with the geese. For the first time, Morgan saw the faint beginnings of a smile on his face. She turned back to the Bible.

"There are three volumes," Martin explained. "This is the one with Ezekiel in it."

He gently turned the thick pages, each one illustrated with extravagant lettering and detailed images that brought the verses alive. Finally, he reached Ezekiel, chapter 37, where the prophet stood with arms stretched out over the dead as they rose from the grave.

Morgan compared it to the image Jake had sent of the Bible in St Louis Cathedral. "That's strange." She showed the picture to Martin. "The symbol in the corner is different between the two copies."

Martin bent closer to look.

Suddenly, the sound of footsteps came from the cloisters outside. A brusque voice called to the monk in Spanish. "Where's the Bible?"

CHAPTER 8

MORGAN TURNED AT THE sound, frowning as she heard the words. Martin looked up, fear in his eyes. This was meant to be a research trip, not an active mission. He wasn't cut out for fighting. Morgan took two swift steps to the door and looked around the edge, catching sight of a group of five men in the cloistered walkway.

It would only be seconds until they reached the room.

She remembered the fight in the church of St Mary in Tabriz, Iran. She and Jake had fought their way out with the Pentecost stone, but Martin wasn't Jake, and she wasn't the fighter she had been back then. The burns on her legs slowed her down, and even though a part of her itched to pull a blade of Toledo steel from the cabinet and give in to the rush of combat, Morgan knew that the best option was to run.

She turned back. "We need to get out of here. Now."

The monk's voice outside directed the men to the room.

Morgan quickly snapped a picture of the Ezekiel page on her smart phone and together, she and Martin slipped out of a side door, pulling it quietly closed behind them.

A couple of monks sat writing in the next room. They looked up at the intrusion, frowning at the unwelcome noise in their sanctuary. Morgan smiled apologetically and hurried to the door, Martin following close behind.

Morgan peered out, glimpsing the men as they walked with determination toward the inner room. The man at the head of the group appeared Spanish or Latino, with dark cropped hair, dark eyes, and skin the color of burnished autumn leaves. He had the muscled body and military bearing of someone who had served, who knew how to handle a weapon.

As the man led his group into the room where the Bible lay, Morgan and Martin ducked down the side of the cloisters and walked quickly back into the central nave of the cathedral.

"We need to get away from here," Morgan said. "There's no way that miserable old monk will keep our presence here a secret."

They left the church and crossed the Plaza del Ayuntamiento, losing themselves in the crowd of tourists that thronged the square. The rain had stopped, but it was still overcast, the sky a gun-metal grey that made the cathedral look even more forbidding.

Once they were well within the crowd, out of sight from the door of the cathedral, Morgan pulled out her smart phone and opened the picture from the Ezekiel page. It showed an open right hand with an eye in the middle, illuminated with iron gall ink and touches of gold leaf.

"It's a *hamsa*, a sign of protection against evil, dating back to early Mesopotamia and the goddess Ishtar or Inanna." Morgan looked up at Martin. "She descended to the Underworld and returned."

He raised an eyebrow. "A kind of resurrection."

Morgan nodded. "It's known as the Hand of Fatima in Muslim culture, but it's also prevalent amongst Sephardi Jews. In Kabbalah, the symbol of the hand can represent the letter *shin*, the first letter of Shaddai, one of the names of God." She frowned. "It seems strange that the *hamsa* would be in a medieval Bible, especially given the history of the Catholic Church here."

"At the time the Bible was created, there was a synagogue here in Toledo," Martin said. "There's still one, well, now it's a museum, but it's not far from here. Only ten minutes' walk."

Morgan thought back to the man in the church, wondering what Jake had gotten her into. She had refused Director Marietti when he had asked her to officially join this mission, but now it seemed she was involved anyway.

She texted Jake with the picture and for a moment considered finishing her involvement here and now. But her curiosity was piqued by the *hamsa*. She smiled to herself, picturing Dinah's face. The knowing look her friend would give her as she headed off on another mission.

The Jews of this city had few to hold their memory high. Morgan would be one of them.

"Let's go to the synagogue now. If those men find the symbol too, they might be heading in the same direction. We need to get ahead of them."

* * *

New Orleans, USA.

Jake woke with a start as his phone vibrated with an incoming text from Morgan. A picture of the Ezekiel page of the Toledo Bible with an unusual *hamsa* the only difference between the Bible pages. Jake knew that Morgan would follow the clue to wherever it might lead next. Part of him wanted to be there with her, memories of their last Spanish mission flickering through his mind. But there were more than enough mysteries here in this blended city of many cultures for him and Naomi to investigate.

He sat up, fighting the heaviness of jet lag that threatened to pull him back under the blanket of sleep. The slats of the shutters let sunlight into the room and outside, Jake could hear the excited chatter of tourists, the clip-clop of carriages as they passed, the strident tones of tour guides explaining the dark history of the French Quarter. He had a quick shower, then headed downstairs to the lobby.

Naomi sat at one of tables, frowning at her laptop. She looked up at his approach.

"I've been researching the links between Catholicism and voodoo, trying to understand how a friar like Père Antoine could have agreed to perform the marriage ceremony for the Voodoo Queen." She raised an eyebrow. "Louisiana voodoo is fascinating."

"You mean there are different kinds? I thought voodoo was just one thing."

Naomi shook her head. "Not at all. Like all religious and spiritual traditions, there are different strands. Louisiana voodoo, or New Orleans voodoo, is different from Haitian voodoo, or Deep Southern hoodoo, although they have aspects in common like ancestor worship and faith in spirits. They all stem from West African beliefs brought over by slaves." Naomi turned her laptop around so Jake could see some of the pictures on screen. Women in trances dancing around a fire, arms raised to the sky. Men with skull-painted faces slashing at their skin, eyes white and bulging. "Like so much surrounding my ancestors, voodoo has been portrayed as evil. Witch doctors casting curses and women possessed by spirits, dancing and singing with abandon."

"Sounds a lot more fun than Christian droning," Jake said.

Naomi frowned. "What do you mean?"

"Imagine a church full of white South African Protestants. A culture that doesn't sing for fun, unenthusiastically intoning bad hymns every Sunday. I used to sneak out to the black church down the street for some joy, even though I knew I'd get a beating for it." Jake shrugged. "Sometimes the strongest faith comes from the oppressed."

Naomi smiled. "Amen to that. These days, many of those practicing voodoo are also faithful Catholics. Singing is common in both traditions, and you'll find the current Voodoo Queen at church on Sunday for Mass. The two beliefs have become entwined over centuries, with voodoo spirits associated with Catholic saints, similar to the way the early church incorporated pagan deities. It's possible Père Antoine appreciated the similarities more than the differences."

Jake thought for a moment. "If Père Antoine was in possession of a relic, something that the Brotherhood protected, and it threatened his community, could he have given it to voodoo practitioners to keep safe? Perhaps something holy to both their Catholic faith and voodoo roots?"

Naomi shrugged. "It's certainly possible. Best to ask those involved in the community. I've tapped into some of my local connections, and we've got a meeting at the Voodoo Museum just a few blocks away." She looked at her watch. "We'd better get going."

They walked out of the hotel along Chartres Street on the edge of the French Quarter, past houses with balconies of wrought iron in faded shades of green. Tall slatted shutters opened over long windows, giving the houses a sense of openness, despite their small size. Some were built in the 'shotgun' style with doors at opposite ends, letting the air flow through during hot summer days.

Jake felt curiously at home amongst the narrow streets, the different languages and the variation in people's faces. He was as mixed-up culturally as any of the residents here, in his beliefs and allegiances, if not his blood.

Born and raised in South Africa, Jake's family had European roots, but he was proudly African, even if people looked at him and denied he could be so because his skin was the wrong color. He had left his homeland after the massacre of his family, joining the military to work for peace, eventually recruited by Director Marietti into ARKANE. In the years since, Jake had seen things that forced him to accept different versions of belief. He had experienced the supernatural over and over again, and now he wondered whether there would ever be a day when he would be able to stop fighting those who wanted to take the world into darkness. He felt a keen desire to know more about voodoo, sensing its practitioners navigated the line between the seen and unseen, as he had done before.

"This is one of the famous haunts of New Orleans." Naomi's voice interrupted Jake's thoughts, and he turned to look up at Saint Mary's Catholic Church with its large building and gardens. Latin words stood out above the door: *Virgini Deiparae Dicatum*. Consecrated to the God-bearing Virgin. "The Ursuline convent. Some say it's responsible for the vampire myth of New Orleans."

Jake looked through the gate into the clipped gardens beyond. "How could a vampire myth possibly come out of a convent?"

"Back in the 1720s," Naomi explained, "this place would have been a hot and mosquito-infested swamp. Not a fun place. There were French settlers, but unsurprisingly, not enough women. So the city's founders asked for prospective wives for the colonists and a series of young women were sent over from the motherland. Each brought a casket with them. When they arrived, several of the girls were pale and gaunt, coughing up blood. Some say they brought vampires from Europe, others say the girls themselves ventured out to suck the blood of the city's residents." Naomi pointed up to the top floor. "The caskets – or coffins – are still up there, the windows nailed shut to stop whatever is in them getting out."

She looked at Jake, and for a moment, Naomi's face was serious. Then she laughed. "Of course, the girls could have just been sick from the journey and ill with tuberculosis."

Jake shook his head. "This place seems to attract both religious and occult energy, mingling the supernatural in new ways. In only a few blocks, you have vampires and zombies, religious relics, and some of the greatest cemeteries in the world."

"Not to mention some seriously nasty murders." Naomi pointed down Governor Nicholls Street as they walked on. "Madame LaLaurie was a Creole socialite, born here in the Spanish colonial period in the late eighteenth century. When a fire brought the authorities to the house, they discovered slaves chained in her attic, their bodies broken by torture. Eyes gouged out, fingernails bloody and torn, flesh sliced away from their skin, their lips sewn together. They say if you sleep there, you can hear the slaves moan in agony." Naomi's eyes were haunted. "But then, you should hear them moan throughout the south. That wasn't exactly the worst injustice carried out down here."

"You certainly bring me to some lovely places," Jake said.

They walked on for several blocks, turning into Dumaine Street toward the New Orleans Historic Voodoo Museum. The entrance was barely noticeable, just a wooden sign hanging above what looked like a modest house. It was rundown with peeling gray paint, rusting railings and boards over the windows.

As they stood outside looking in, one of the shutters creaked open, a thin curl of smoke winding up from the shadowed figure inside.

CHAPTER 9

Toledo, Spain.

MORGAN AND MARTIN WALKED through the narrow streets of the old city, emerging behind the El Greco Museum. Tiles on the ground cemented between stones, fixed to walls, or hidden in corners marked the edges of the Jewish Quarter. Tiny menorahs on blue porcelain, and *chai*, the Hebrew word for life, inscribed on smooth white tiles that stood out against the cobbles of the old streets. Tourists walked by, looking in the shop windows at *mezuzahs* and Star of David pendants, but those who knew the history of the area looked down at the ground searching for the tiles as a reminder of the vibrant community who once lived here.

They passed down an alleyway with walls made from fragments of Roman bricks built into new foundations, eventually arriving at the Sinagoga del Tránsito. Morgan and Martin paid the entrance fee, picked up an information leaflet and walked inside.

Morgan stood in the main hall, looking up and around her. The front wall featured a delicate carved frieze with slender columns and a floral pattern in the Nasrid-style reminiscent of the Alhambra palace in Granada. High windows above allowed light to touch the carved Hebrew phrases that ran around the walls. Words from the Psalms, a promise that those who had died here would never be forgotten.

She walked over to a display board of information, reading that the synagogue had been built in 1356. After the expulsion of the Jews from Spain in 1492, it became a church then eventually a museum in the early 1900s. It now remained as a testament to the people who had lost their homes under the Alhambra Decree, also known as the Edict of Expulsion, made by the Catholic monarchs of Spain, Isabella I of Castile and Ferdinand II of Aragon. Many of Spain's Jews converted because of persecution and pogroms, but the rest chose to leave rather than betray their faith.

"Incredibly, the Alhambra Decree was only revoked in 1968 following the Second Vatican Council," Martin said, his voice low out of respect for the place. "And it was only in 2014 that the government passed a law allowing dual citizenship to Sephardi Jewish descendants as compensation."

"But that won't bring back the people who once thrived here," Morgan said. "We can't change history, and the diaspora was a curse and a blessing, as the verse in Deuteronomy says. Jews live all over the world now. They cannot be wiped out as those monarchs and so many others intended. Now, let's find this *hamsa*."

A second-floor gallery stretched the length of the top floor above the main hall. It would have been reserved for women, segregated from men during services, but now it was part of the museum. They climbed the stairs and walked into the gallery.

Morgan gazed into the cabinets, examining the meager offerings left behind, a tiny glimpse of the once vibrant Jewish community. *Mezuzahs*, a small menorah, old letters written in Hebrew, and ritual objects for a *bris* – but no *hamsa*.

There was nothing of importance here. It was a dead end.

* * *

New Orleans, USA.

A voice came from inside the Voodoo Museum, as a curl of smoke escaped the shutters.

"What you waiting for, *cher*? Come on in here."

Naomi pulled open the door and walked inside, Jake following behind. The front room of the house was a little shop crammed full of voodoo souvenirs. It was dark with the shutters so tightly closed, but Jake could just make out gris-gris charms, fetish dolls, vials of potion, and books on the voodoo history of New Orleans. The line between real belief and tourist tack was hard to navigate in this eclectic city. While voodoo had its true practitioners, there was clearly a commercial side. It was no different to Catholic places of pilgrimage like Lourdes, where plastic Mary figurines filled with 'holy water' were sold to the faithful on every inch of the pilgrimage route.

An old African-American woman sat smoking a fat, rolled-up cigarette, sweet-smelling smoke curling around her. She was thin, her flesh tight against her skull, a bright green headscarf wrapped around her white hair. The woman regarded Jake with curiosity.

"You've seen him, boy." Her voice was croaky, but there was a hint of steel under her words.

Jake's heart pounded in his chest as he met the old woman's keen gaze. She pointed up with her cigarette to a dark figure painted above the tourist shelves. A skeletal man etched in charcoal, a top hat on his head. Baron Samedi, *loa* of the dead.

"He may have worn a different face, but you've seen him. And you will see him again."

The old woman focused her attention on Naomi. "But

you, child, you have a new soul. You may yet see." The old woman tilted her head to one side. "Or you may be called by the bones to the world of the dead."

The old woman lapsed into silence. She took a long drag on her cigarette, the sweet-smelling haze filling the room. Jake felt the air shift around her, and suddenly he saw beyond the tacky trinkets in front of him, sensing an older power here, a deeper current swirling beneath.

He opened his mouth to speak, but Naomi stepped forward. "OK, well, thank you for your welcome." She opened her handbag and brought out a piece of paper. "We're here to meet Fabienne Beauvais."

"What do you want with my granddaughter?"

The sound of footsteps came from a doorway. A lithe young woman walked out of the museum rooms beyond. Neat dreadlocks hung down to her mid-back, tied with a silk scarf of brilliant turquoise that matched her t-shirt. Her eye makeup was perfectly applied, her lips dark with a crimson shade. She was a modern incarnation of mixed-race New Orleans, but there was more than a trace of the old woman in her features.

"You welcoming our guests properly, Mamere?" The young woman held her hand out. "I'm Fabienne, welcome. You must be Naomi."

"And I'm Jake." Jake held his hand out and shook hands with Fabienne. Their eyes met, and he felt a jolt of attraction arc between them. He dropped her hand and took a step back.

The old woman cackled with laughter. She pushed herself up to her feet, stubbing her cigarette out. "You show this one everything, child. He can handle it."

The old woman shuffled out the door and into the sunshine.

Fabienne rolled her eyes. "Please forgive my grandmother. She's stuck in the old ways. Doesn't understand the need to bring in money at the same time as respecting the spirits. But, I think we can do both here in New Orleans. Come on through to the museum, and I'll show you."

Fabienne led Jake and Naomi through a series of rooms in the old house packed full of voodoo sacred objects and offerings from the faithful – or just the superstitious. The rooms were claustrophobic, every inch of wall space and most of the floor covered with dusty and faded things.

"You asked how our Catholic faith integrates with voodoo. Well, here's one example." Fabienne pointed at a table where an old Bible lay open to the book of Proverbs, chapter 25. It was covered in offerings, a copper key, several rings, coins, a little toy in the shape of a crocodile, a Milky Way chocolate bar, photos of loved ones, dollar bills, lipstick and face cream, a higgledy-piggledy mess of every day detritus left as offerings to the spirits.

A skull with a black top hat, cigarettes and money spilling from its eye sockets sat next to the Bible. Baron Samedi once more.

Further on, an altar as large as a dining table sat with a statue of the Virgin Mary in pride of place, surrounded by other saints and an icon showing Jesus of the Sacred Heart, a red orb shining luminous in his chest. The altar was piled high with offerings, bright beads from Mardi Gras, vials of dark liquid, letters and business cards, sweets and money.

Fabienne gestured toward the altar. "Our faiths are deeply entwined, as sure as my blood is both African and American." She pointed to the images of the saints. "Papa Legba holds the keys to the underworld and is associated with St Peter and his keys to the gates of heaven. Some say roosters are sacrificed to Papa Legba because St Peter denied Christ three times before the rooster crowed. Snakes are worshipped in voodoo with Damballah, and he is often represented by St Patrick, and also Moses. Patrick drove the serpents out of Ireland and Moses held up the brazen serpent in the desert. Some say that eating flesh and drinking blood is part of voodoo, but of course, it's actually related to the Catholic Mass, when transubstantiation turns bread and wine into the real flesh and blood of Christ." Fabienne shrugged. "You can see how people might get confused."

She led them on into another room. The skull of a horse painted with a white cross hung next to femur bones tied with black ribbon. A mummified cat lay on a shelf, desiccated skin tight against its rigid bones, its head thrust toward the heavens.

"Black cat juju," Fabienne explained. "Used to protect the home against evil spirits around the Day of the Dead."

Jake noticed a piece of wood as long as an arm bone, spiked with nails hammered into every inch. To some, it may have looked like a weapon, but Jake knew it for what it really was. He had seen such sacrificial objects in Africa. For every sin, a nail was driven in, each blow of the hammer sending evil into the wood rather than the person who committed the crime.

"You can see the mixed mythology in so many ways." Fabienne pointed at an image of a half-man, half-alligator. "The *rougarou* is said by some to be the *loup-garou* of the French werewolf tradition, but here in the bayou, it has the head of an alligator." She smiled. "We like to localize our dark secrets."

Her words were light, but Jake sensed something else beneath. The museum may have been designed to extract tourist dollars, but there was truth underlying it. Myths had wound themselves together here over generations, and evil committed in the Deep South compounded whatever spirits lay beneath the earth, bloodshed bringing ancient nightmares to life.

They finished the tour of the museum and returned to the first room. Naomi walked back to the Bible, her fingers tracing the words of the text.

"When we were at the cathedral, we discovered that Père Antoine had baptized Marie Laveau. Have you heard that story?"

Fabienne nodded. "Of course. There's no conflict between Catholicism and voodoo in our tradition, only that manufactured by those who wish to discredit us. The voodoo statement of faith includes belief in the spirits and all things visible and invisible, the gods of Africa, and the saints of the Catholic Church."

She led them into a narrow corridor, stopping by a painting of a light-skinned woman with dark eyes, her hair wrapped in an ivory-colored headscarf with red trim. "This is Marie Laveau, proud Catholic and Voodoo Queen. Père Antoine baptized her and presided over her marriage in his later years. Some say that they were scandalously close, but perhaps they merely talked of religious and spiritual matters. When the Catholic authorities tried to remove him, there is a rumor that he gave Marie something to hide, something he wanted to keep out of the hands of certain factions in the Church. Some say what he gave her is still protected by the Creole voodoo community."

"Do you know what it was?" Jake asked.

Fabienne shook her head, a glimmer of fear in her eyes. "There are only rumors, and to be honest, I'm done with the old superstitions. It's time to bring our beliefs into a modern age. But my grandmother, Albertine, is one of the elders." She looked at Jake. "She clearly saw something in you, so perhaps she will talk further about it. But it would need to be away from the city. She won't talk of such things here. She believes it's polluted now, and the *loa* will not come to her in this manufactured world."

"Where do we need to go?"

"She lives in the bayou. I can take you to her tonight."

CHAPTER 10

New Orleans, USA.

As they walked away from the museum, Naomi felt a rising dread at the thought of heading into the bayou later. She was a city girl, raised in the high-rise jungle of New York, where predators wore human masks as they stalked the shadowed streets. She knew how to deal with them well enough, but she had experienced little of adventure in the wild. She was more at home with books, even sleeping in her tiny office when she was deep into research.

The stacks of the local library had been her escape from the poverty and despair of her neighborhood growing up. She read of heroes who roamed the African savannah and turned the pages as intrepid heroines hunted evildoers across ancient cities. She reveled in the cathartic thrill of story, but she also loved closing the book and returning to her ordered world where she could control her surroundings.

But Naomi couldn't control everything, and when her little sister, Esther, died suddenly of meningitis, her parents poured everything into their remaining daughter. They worked two jobs each to pay for her education, both of them urging her on to forge a path in academia, both of them revering books and knowledge over physical pursuits that might harm her in some way. Living as if wrapped in cotton wool was a small price to pay for her parents' peace of mind.

Joining ARKANE with her PhD in Linguistics enabled Naomi to play a part in the adventures of agents in the field, but usually from the safe confines of her office in the basement of the United Nations building. There were over 800 languages spoken in New York alone, so she had no shortage of projects, but her time with Jake on the hunt for the relic of the angel had given her a new perspective. She'd experienced the city she thought she knew from another angle, navigating tunnels beneath the streets, exploring the island of the dead – and killing a man who almost finished her first.

Naomi still dreamed of his face, snarling as he fought with her, eyes wide with shock as he died, but the experience only made her want to get out of the office more often. She had faced fear and death and made it through to the other side. The only way to become a better agent was to face it again. So when this mission had come up, she'd asked to be assigned. There had to be a purpose to her life beyond studying books and artifacts in the depths of the ARKANE offices.

She turned her head to look at Jake beside her as they headed through the streets of the French Quarter back to the hotel. He was quiet, lost in thought, but in his eyes, she saw a glimmer of excitement. He was going to the bayou, with or without her, and she would not be left behind.

* * *

Toledo, Spain.

Morgan walked over to the edge of the gallery where it overlooked the main hall of the synagogue. From this high up, she could see the Hebrew script more clearly. It curved around the edge of the wall near the ceiling, each letter in pure white against a dark background, as if floating against the expanse of the cosmos. It made Morgan think of her father bent over his Torah meditating on the shapes of the letters, looking past surface meaning to allegorical interpretation according to his Kabbalistic belief.

The memory jogged something she had glimpsed in the museum below, a brief notice about the history of Kabbalah in Toledo during the Middle Ages.

She spun around to Martin, who had wandered over to look at the finials on a Torah crown.

He looked up at her sudden movement. "What is it?"

"Remember after the Gates of Hell mission, when I brought back my father's journals from Israel?"

Martin nodded. "Yes, of course, I scanned and archived them as you requested." He tapped his pocket. "I can access them all through the portal on my phone."

Morgan walked over to the long bench at the end of the gallery and patted the seat next to her. "Right, we need to search them for any mention of Toledo. If there was a scholar of Kabbalah here, then my father would have known him."

Martin sat more than a few inches away, enough to preserve his personal space, and Morgan respectfully didn't lean over, waiting for him to access the scanned journals. His fingers moved incredibly fast over the keypad as a frown deepened between his eyebrows.

After a few minutes, he smiled and held the phone out for her to see. "Here, Rabbi Jonah Ben-Avraham. It looks like your father met him several times at Kabbalah conferences."

Morgan stood up and straightened her clothes. "Right then, time to go see if he's still in town. You stay here."

She headed back downstairs to the entrance and explained her family connection to the volunteer on the desk.

He nodded in recognition of the name. "Of course, Rabbi Jonah still lives in Toledo, just around the corner in the heart of the Jewish Quarter. He doesn't get many visitors these days. Do you want me to call him?"

"Yes, please. I know my father would have wanted me to pay my respects."

The man dialed and spoke in Hebrew for a few minutes, then put the phone down and turned back to Morgan.

"The Rabbi says he remembers your father and would be happy to meet you. If you could wait in the gallery upstairs, he'll be along shortly."

Morgan returned to the gallery and sat together with Martin. It wasn't long before slow footsteps ascended the stairs and an old man walked in. His brown corduroy suit had seen better days, but it gave the Rabbi a professorial air. He wore a white *kippah* on his balding head with a blue Star of David in the middle that matched his piercing eyes. The Rabbi might have been past his heyday of Kabbalah scholarship, but Morgan knew she wouldn't want to face him across a debating chamber.

She stood up as he entered and walked over to greet him. "Rabbi Jonah, thank you for meeting us. I'm Morgan Sierra, and this is my colleague, Martin Klein. I think you knew my father."

The Rabbi reached out and clasped Morgan's outstretched hand in both of his. "Shalom and welcome to you both. I knew Leon in better times and I was sorry to hear of his passing. He taught me much of Kabbalah." He released Morgan's hand and looked at her more closely. "I see him in your features, but more than that. You have his curiosity, too."

Morgan pulled out her phone. "It's curiosity that brings us here, actually." She scrolled to the picture from Ezekiel and turned it round so he could see. "This is a page from the illustrated Toledo Bible in the cathedral. Do you know why the *hamsa* might be on a Christian manuscript?"

Rabbi Jonah leaned closer, gazing at the figures around the edges of the page. The skeletons rising from the grave.

The prophet with his outstretched arm summoning the power of God. When he looked at Morgan again, there were clouds in his blue eyes as if he could see a storm coming.

"The book of Ezekiel is from Jewish scripture, of course," the Rabbi said. "But the *Hand* of Ezekiel is something else. Quite the legend in these parts, although perhaps there is more to it than just a story."

He paused and for a moment, Morgan didn't know whether he would speak of what he knew. Then the Rabbi sighed. "The *hamsa* can represent the five-fold books of the Torah. It can be a gesture of friendship, of healing and protection. But here in this city of three cultures, it represents a physical object."

The Rabbi shuffled slowly toward the end of the gallery. In the last cabinet, a wooden chest stood behind glass. It was nothing to look at, crumbling and mostly rotted away, not worth a second glance.

The Rabbi slid the glass across, opened the chest and pulled out a folded piece of cloth, turned yellow with age. "For the sake of your father, I share this with you."

He unwrapped it to reveal an old key, the cuts deep and jagged.

"In 1492," he explained, "the Jews who refused to convert locked their doors and left their homes. Everything was taken from them, but some kept the keys. Over hundreds of years, few people have returned, but some of the keys were handed down, and some places from that time still stand. This key was given to me by an American who said it would unlock a secret that could threaten the Church itself. He didn't understand what that meant, but he was the last of his line with no one else to leave the key with, so he left it here with us."

Morgan nodded. "For we are family wherever we are in the world. My father used to say that."

The Rabbi smiled. "It remains true."

"But what does it unlock?" Martin asked.

Rabbi Jonah reached back into the chest and pulled out a hand-drawn map of old Toledo. A *hamsa* symbol lay over the end of one street.

"This house has been in the same Christian family since 1492. It's said that their ancestors were part of the Inquisition and they picked the best houses and the best land when the Jews were expelled. They also have one of the most extensive private collections of holy relics in all of Spain."

"But surely the key can't be for a modern house?"

The Rabbi shook his head. "No, but there is a vault where the relics are held, inside the old house. Some say what is kept down there is both Jewish and Christian. Some even say it can raise the dead."

CHAPTER 11

IT WAS DUSK BY the time Morgan and Martin left the synagogue and headed toward the house marked with a *hamsa* upon the map.

The old city was quiet away from the throng of tourists. There were few street lamps, but Morgan was happy to walk in the shadows, where memories of those driven out still haunted the stones in layers of bloody history. She clutched the key in her hand, ready to enter the old house as a representative of a Jewish family beyond the grave. But more than that, she was curious to see what the relic room held.

Morgan wasn't actually Jewish – her mother had been a Christian – but she was raised in Israel with her father, a Kabbalist Jew. The Catholic faith still puzzled her with its extravagant images of saints with the faces of the dead instead of an ineffable God whose name could not even be spoken. For Jews, a dead body should be buried whole, not cut into bits and worshipped as something holy. Yet Spain was full of these relics, body parts of martyrs kept in boxes, hidden beneath altars, consecrating the ground they lay upon. These saints interceded with God on behalf of those still living, and it seemed to have worked for the Catholic monarchs in 1492. He certainly hadn't been on the side of the Jews back then.

Turning down increasingly narrow streets, Morgan and Martin finally reached the door of the house of the *hamsa*. The front wall had been rebuilt with modern bricks, but an inlaid stone tablet told of its historic value. It had a thick wooden door etched with a cross, on which rested a knocker in the shape of a sword. An electronic keypad sat next to it on the side wall. Like Toledo itself, the house was a mixture of medieval and modern life.

"What if someone's in there?" Martin whispered, his back against the stone wall.

Morgan turned to reassure him. "It's OK. The family are away for the summer, so it should be empty."

"Maybe we should wait. Get permission?"

Morgan thought back to the Latino man in the cathedral, his muscular body, the determination on his face. "We don't have time."

She lifted the sword knocker and banged it down. The sound reverberated through the house. But there were no footsteps, no sounds within. Morgan knocked again. They waited another minute before she stepped back.

"Over to you."

Martin pulled an electronic device from his bag and attached it over the keypad. "I still don't know if we should be doing this."

He turned it on. With a click and a clunk, the door opened into a grand hallway.

It was clear that the family didn't really live here. The place was pristine, all stark minimalist furniture and modern art with no sense of being a home.

"It looks like they gutted the original building," Martin noted as they walked inside.

Morgan stopped by one of the inner door frames, her arms spanning the size of the walls either side. "But look. This thicker wall is from an older time. They must have constructed around the medieval house, adding a modern skin."

She wandered further through the labyrinth of rooms, Martin following behind until they reached a medieval door studded with metal divots and an elaborate keyhole. Morgan pulled out the ancient key and fitted it into the lock, sliding it inside with ease.

"It fits," she said in wonder, amazed that it would really work after so long. But then the craftsmanship of the Toledo metalworkers was renowned in the medieval world, so why shouldn't their locks last for hundreds of years?

She turned the key and pushed open the door.

It was dark, but there was a curious sense of abundance in the space beyond. Morgan flicked on a lamp, casting a golden light over what lay inside.

Ornate carved wooden cabinets stretched up to the ceiling on all four walls of the room, each glass-fronted to show what lay within – religious relics, the bones and blood of the dead.

Martin turned slowly to take it all in, his eyes wide. "This is incredible. I've never seen so many reliquaries in a private collection. There must be hundreds, if not thousands, of relics in here."

The macabre spectacle made Morgan uneasy. Whose bones were these really? She leaned closer to one of the cabinets. A skull lay on a bed of crimson cloth surrounded by faded silk flowers. Above it, a femur bone stood in a leg-shaped golden reliquary inscribed with the name of an obscure saint. Next to it, a row of tiny boxes with slivers of bone and vials of blood within. And so it went on. In every cabinet, there were more bones, more body parts, more congealed blood.

Morgan frowned. "Why would the Toledo Bible lead here? Why the *hamsa* symbol?"

"What about that?" Martin pointed at an altar in the middle of the room. A golden case rested on top with glass panes on all four sides so the relic could be seen inside. He bent to look closer. "It's a metacarpal, a finger bone, and look there." A red wax seal capped the end of the bone. "It's a vial, a relic that's also a container of some kind." He grinned with excitement. "This could be the link. In the West African tradition, a certain powder can bring the dead to life."

"And Ezekiel stretched out his hand to summon the dead from the grave," Morgan continued, recalling the image in the illuminated Bible. "So that could explain the idea of a finger bone."

"Perhaps this will tell us more." Martin turned to the book that rested next to the case. "It's a Book of Days." He flicked through the pages, skimming the text quickly.

Morgan watched him, wondering at how his brain worked. Some at ARKANE wondered if Martin was on the autism spectrum, some called him a socially awkward data geek, but regardless of labels, he was one of the most brilliant researchers she'd ever met.

A minute later, Martin pointed to a page covered in dense handwriting. "Here. It says that something was smuggled out from the dungeons of the Inquisition, a secret hidden within the Hand of Ezekiel." He looked up. "This is it."

"But it's only one finger," Morgan said. "Where's the rest of it?"

A sharp banging suddenly echoed through the house. She turned toward the door. "They're here."

Morgan hated to run again, but they had no choice. This wasn't an official mission, they had no right to be in this house, and there was no one here who could fight next to her. She had no weapon, never even thinking that she might need one on a research trip to look at a Bible.

Martin pulled open his backpack and put the reliquary inside. He grabbed the book and stuffed that in as well. "Let's go."

They slipped out of the room, and Morgan took one last look at the medieval door, thinking of the Jewish family who had once owned the key. They wouldn't have wanted their old home to be full of dead flesh, holy relics of the faith that almost destroyed them. But perhaps she was one step closer to righting that ancient wrong.

She and Martin slipped out of the back door as they heard the entrance forced open with some kind of battering ram rather than an electronic key. The men didn't care about being heard or seen, clearly determined to get what they wanted regardless of destruction in their wake. Something to keep in mind, Morgan thought. Perhaps it wasn't the last she would see of the Latino man and his team.

*   *   *

New Orleans, USA.

Luis sat at his desk, drumming his fingers on the table next to the bone box, every minute like an hour as he waited for news from Toledo. The files of experiments on the shelves of his office mocked him with their repeated failure. They were so close.

His phone rang. Finally, an incoming video call from Julio.

Luis tapped to accept the call. "Did you find the relic?"

But even as he spoke, Luis's heart sank in his chest as he saw the expression on Julio's face.

"The Bible had a Jewish symbol in it which led us to a synagogue. An old Rabbi tried to tell us there was nothing to find, but after some – persuasion – he told us of a family who kept a relic room. We're in the shrine now, but there are so many bones here. I don't know which one you want."

Julio held up the phone on video mode and slowly turned around, taking in the expanse of walls filled with relics. Luis squinted at the screen as he tried to process the sheer number of them. It was magnificent, a real treasure trove, but Julio could hardly bring everything back. After all, most relics were just dead bone, whereas what he sought was so much more.

"Is there anything in pride of place? Anything on an altar?"

Julio walked forward, the video screen focusing on a table with a rumpled white altar-cloth marked with lines of dust.

"Someone has been here already and taken the relic." Julio's voice was low, a note of threat in his tone. "I'll get it back for you, señor, I promise."

Luis put his head in his hands, trying to calm his rising panic. "Did the Rabbi mention anyone else who visited today?"

Julio shook his head. "I didn't ask him. Sorry, boss. I wasn't thinking."

"Get back there and find the security camera footage. I want a picture of whoever was in that museum before you."

Luis ended the call, willing Julio to find whoever had beat him to the relic. It was only one finger bone, but he needed all five.

Suddenly, a red light flashed on the wall of the office. His phone began to ring with a tone reserved for only one reason.

Elena.

Luis rose to his feet and hurried as fast as he could to the elevator, down, and then back toward the medical suite. He shuffled, half-running, panting as he rushed down the corridor.

The door to Elena's room was open. The sound of raised voices within. The high-pitched beeping of medical equipment.

Luis stood at the door watching as the doctors worked on his daughter, her petite frame covered in bony growths, the ravages of their shared disease. She was intubated, sedated, her face crumpling into peace as the drugs took her beyond pain.

Helplessness rose within him. He had the top medical team, access to the best drugs and cutting-edge technology. And yet, if he didn't find this miracle, his daughter would die. And his world would end with her.

"The latest growth is crushing her left lung," one of the doctors said. "Every breath is difficult and painful. She was gasping and in agony, so we sedated her for now. What do you want us to do?"

I should let her go. It's what she wants. Luis banged his fist on the door frame as his frustration spilled over. "Keep her alive as long as you can."

Once they had stabilized her, Luis sat down by Elena's bedside and took her hand in his. Her skin was warm, and the machines beeped to the rhythm of her pulse. He smoothed hair from her forehead, tucked the sheet around her. His daughter was alive. He would keep her that way.

His phone vibrated with an incoming text from Julio.

Luis opened it to see a picture of a woman with strong, angular features and Hispanic or perhaps Israeli coloring. Her dark curls were tied back, and she had striking blue eyes with a curious slash of violet in the right one.

Behind her was a man with rough-cut blonde hair, wire-rim glasses, his face scrunched into a frown. The man would look more at home in a lab, but the woman held herself like someone who knew how to fight.

But then Luis looked again.

There was something beneath her strength. He recognized the way she held her body, an echo of the way he held his own. The posture of someone in physical pain. This woman had a weakness.

CHAPTER 12

Madrid, Spain.

MARTIN SAT IN THE corner of the drab hotel room reading the Toledo Book of Days. The modern city streets teemed with life outside the window, cars honking, the bustle of commuters, but he seemed oblivious, his mind anchored into centuries gone by. Morgan sat by the window, remaining as still as possible to allow him to stay deep in concentration. She watched as the frown deepened between his eyebrows. He reached up and ran his hand through the shock of blonde hair, tugging it so hard that it stood up at all angles. She knew that Martin would be itching to get this knowledge into the ARKANE database as soon as possible. He had a scanner back in London that would photograph the text and index it entirely, but for now, they would have to make do with reading it the old-fashioned way.

The relic sat in its glass case on a rickety desk by the wall, out of place here in the modern world. The gold leaf looked fake. It was too bright, too ornate. The bone inside was plain, and yet it held the real treasure.

"Incredible!" Martin said suddenly, jumping to his feet in excitement, bobbing up and down on his toes. "This journal has been passed down through those in the Brotherhood of the Breath, dedicated to preserving the secret in case the Church ever needed it, but also to keep it out of the hands of those who might use it in the wrong way."

He paced the room, one hand clutching the book, the other sketching in the air, his face alive with passion. Morgan couldn't help but be drawn into his story as Martin continued. "It began with the Inquisition. A secret brought from Equatorial Guinea by a zealous monk, a series of powders that when mixed together could bring the dead back to life, used in conjunction with specific words of power. Recalling the verses of Ezekiel about raising the dead, the Brotherhood didn't destroy the powder but hid it within relics of finger bones to represent the Hand. They doubted, but they couldn't destroy something that might have been a sign from God."

Morgan went to the desk and picked up the reliquary. "It makes sense. Relics are so common in the Catholic world that they could hide these in plain sight. But where are the rest?"

Martin frowned. "That's the puzzle. The Brotherhood entrusted it to five of their number who took them to different parts of the Catholic world over the years of Empire."

"Does the book list their names?"

Martin shook his head. "No such luck. But it does give the name of a missionary college in Mexico where a Spanish priest arrived in 1750 carrying one of them. He was sent from the Spanish island of Majorca."

A smile dawned on Morgan's face as she considered his words.

Martin looked at her with suspicion. "You're not thinking ..."

Morgan grinned. "It's only an hours' flight, and I've heard Majorca is beautiful. I'm sure Jake would want us to follow the clues and find the name of the priest. The only question is whether you're coming with me?"

* * *

New Orleans, USA.

The sky was dark, heavy with rain clouds as Jake and Naomi walked out of the hotel, dressed for an excursion into the wetlands, carrying dry-bags with head-lamps, rain jackets and a change of clothes.

Fabienne sat outside in a four-wheel-drive truck, having changed from her urban clothes into faded denim, transforming the city girl into someone they hoped would lead them through the labyrinthine waterways of the Louisiana bayou.

Jake climbed into the back, leaving Naomi to ride up front. He gazed out of the window as they left the city, the highway overlooking gritty apartment buildings, strip malls and rundown neighborhoods. They passed one of the levees and Jake remembered the apocalyptic scenes in the aftermath of Hurricane Katrina. It was hard to imagine how the city had survived, and yet it rose again from the mud and ruins, its people still playing jazz and singing. New Orleans was itself a resurrection.

After the inevitable traffic jams, they emerged from the city limits, heading south to finally arrive at the Jean Lafitte National Historical Park and Preserve.

Fabienne parked up beside a gate separating the road from a line of live oak and black walnut trees. Nature encroached on the concrete, lichen and moss inching its way out, clawing a foothold into the constructed world. The wild ruled this place and would reclaim its land just as soon as people turned their backs on it.

Fabienne climbed out and grabbed her backpack from the trunk along with a cooler bag. Jake raised an eyebrow. "We having a picnic out there?"

"Spicy chicken wings. Grandma's favorite. I have rum too. Thought it might help the evening go well." Fabienne pointed down the track. "We walk from here, and pick up kayaks to go deeper into the bayou."

Jake felt a trickle of sweat run down his spine as he emerged from the car. It was hot and sultry out of the air conditioning, the air muggy with the approaching storm. He helped Naomi with her gear and then hefted his own pack onto his back. "Does your grandma live a long way out?"

Fabienne gave a half-smile, her expression guarded. "She tends to keep herself to herself. I'm only bringing you out here because she saw something in you. Perhaps she'll help you with what you seek." She shrugged. "Perhaps not."

As Fabienne led them through the gate and down a pathway through the trees, Jake noticed that the young woman was different out here. Her expertly applied makeup had been removed, but it was more than that. She played the forward-thinking city girl with ease back in the French Quarter, but it was clear that the bayou was her real home.

They were soon out of sight of the car, walking under live oak trees hung with a tangle of Spanish moss down a winding path to the water's edge. Fabienne pointed to a wooden shack with boarded-up windows.

"That's it. I hope you're ready for a paddle."

She unlocked the door to reveal four kayaks hung on racks, battered but useable. They each lifted one down and carried them out to the bayou.

Fabienne quickly launched hers and waited out on the muddy-green channel. She leaned her head back and looked up at the swirling clouds above.

"The storm is close now. We should get moving. We have a ways to go."

Naomi struggled to get into her kayak. Jake went over to help her steady it.

"I'm not sure this is such a good idea," she whispered,

her eyes darting out to Fabienne. "I've only kayaked once before. I won't be able to go very fast. Are we really going to trust her to lead us through the swamp? What if we get lost? What if –"

Jake put his hand over hers. "It's OK. You're going to be alright. I've done a lot of kayaking, and this will only be calm water and smooth paddling, don't you worry. This might be our only chance to find out more about the relic and the history behind Marie Laveau and Père Antoine. But you can stay behind if you want to. I'll go with Fabienne."

Naomi shook her head. "No, I want to come. Just … don't leave me behind."

Jake leaned in and gave her a quick hug. "Of course not. We're partners on this mission. Partners don't leave each other behind." He chuckled. "Remember, you were bored in the office, and this is about as far away from paperwork as you can get."

Naomi paddled out hesitantly to join Fabienne and as Jake watched her go, he thought of Morgan, remembered how she had never left him behind. Even when he had been near death from snakebite in the Negev desert in Israel, she had made sure he was safe. He wished that she were here now, rather than half a world away.

Jake swiftly launched his kayak and pushed out onto the slow-moving waters. The air was damp, and he found himself quickly soaked with sweat as they paddled out along the bank and into the labyrinth of channels that led into the heart of the reserve. The Louisiana bayou was a unique ecosystem made up of tidal waters and sluggish rivers, marshy lakes and wetland areas. The water was brackish, a mix of salt water and fresh, and the faint smell of the sea was just noticeable under the stink of rotting vegetation and the heavy perfume of tropical flowers. It was entropy in action, life and death cycling ever faster as the creatures of the bayou lived out their allotted span.

"Climate change and human development have ravaged this area," Fabienne noted as they paddled on. "Hurricanes and tropical storms as well as agricultural runoff and chemical spills have led to the destruction of nearly two thousand miles of Louisiana's coastal wetlands."

She paused, her paddle motionless on her lap as she listened to the birdsong around them – the ascending call of the Northern Parula and the warble of the Yellow-breasted Chat. "It's a mixed blessing, I guess. The constant shifting of what is earth and what is water means there will be no new development since it could all be destroyed so quickly. It keeps those who want stability, an unshifting foundation, away."

"And your grandmother?" Naomi asked.

Fabienne shrugged. "She understands that nothing stays the same, and she's closer to life and death out here. Closer to the *loa*, the spirits. Those who came from Africa, and those native to this area. She listens to them all."

Jake saw a flicker of longing on Fabienne's face, perhaps a desire for such surety in faith.

She led them out into a channel past low-lying islands, under twisting limbs of cypress trees with canopies of gray-green Spanish moss that trailed into the water. Fabienne lifted some up with her paddle.

"It's not actually moss and it's not from Spain, although it was named after the beards of the Spanish Conquistadors. It's not a parasite, either. It grows on healthy trees in tropical swampland, and both live and thrive together. The way we should live with the land."

The call of birds filled the air as dusk fell. A blue heron stood at the water's edge fishing, picking its way through the shallows on long, spindly legs. A sudden splash of frogs jumping.

"You can live well in the bayou," Fabienne said, as they paddled on through the bright green expanse of duckweed dotted with deep purple flowers of Louisiana Iris and the white fronds of the Spider Lily. "Crawfish, shrimp, catfish, alligator sometimes. The tourists pay handsomely for what we 'poor folk' get out of the swamp." She laughed. "Life has always found a way here. The Choctaw Native American people inhabited the Louisiana bayou for centuries, then slaves escaped out here, outlaws, immigrants who couldn't find another way to live. They all came. Sometimes hiding is the best way to protect yourself." She paused and then said softly. "Those who practice voodoo understand this, and so the true rituals are performed here, away from the prying eyes of the city."

"I thought this was a protected area?" Naomi asked, more relaxed now she was into the rhythm of paddling. "How come your grandmother lives here?"

"Jean Lafitte is a nature reserve, but there are hiking trails, and kayaks are allowed through the hardwood forests, swamps and marsh. Ecotourism companies bring money to the area, but they only venture into certain parts. We're going further in. To the secret places."

Fabienne looked over at Jake, and he saw a dark promise there. Of what, he was unsure. She paddled on, her lithe figure moving as one with the kayak. "I don't know what Grandma sees in you, but I sure hope you're ready for whatever she chooses to reveal."

They reached a narrow channel where the waterway turned more into swamp and clouds of mosquitos hung over stagnant water. In places, they had to jerk the kayaks forward with their hips, unable to even paddle in the shallow water. Jake angled his kayak around the cypress knees jutting out from the water like severed limbs clutching for the sky, surrounded by choking duckweed. He pushed on through the tight passage, staying close to Naomi to make sure she wasn't left behind. Her paddling had slowed, but she persisted, her jaw set with determination.

They were deep into the swamp when Jake sensed a shift in atmosphere. The sky was purple with streaks of gold and scarlet, turning the reflective waters around them to the color of blood. The encroaching storm crackled around them and as night fell, the hunters emerged.

He looked up to see the silhouette of a huge barred owl dive down to snatch a small rodent from the water's edge. He could almost feel the rush of air from its wings and imagined its sharp beak ripping into the tiny body.

Although the bayou was a long way from the plains of Africa where he had grown up, Jake sensed the same thrill of nature here, the fine line between life and death. He understood why Fabienne and her grandmother, Albertine, would spend their time out here away from the city. It was so close and yet so far away from the tourist thoroughfares of the French Quarter, where partygoers drank to escape their mundane lives. The carnival spirit raged, whirling in ever-faster turns, but out here, the energy was slow-moving, yet far more powerful. This land was hard-won and could be taken back by the gods of storm and chaos in a heartbeat. Death walked close with life here. Maybe that's why he felt so at home.

They rounded a bend in the channel and emerged into a wider stream. For a moment, Jake thought it must be full of logs.

Then he realized what they actually were.

Scaly bumps of alligator backs in the water. Some small, only as long as his arm, but others were several feet long.

A colossal head pushed up through the duckweed, green petals caught between its scales as reptilian eyes focused on potential prey. Its gigantic tail thrashed in the water, propelling the beast toward the kayaks.

CHAPTER 13

Palma, Majorca, Spain.

THE PLANE BANKED OVER the ocean as it came into land at Palma on Majorca, the largest island in the Balearics off the east coast of Spain. The Mediterranean Sea glistened turquoise and silver in the early morning sun, and the white sails of yachts dotted the harbor below. Morgan could just glimpse the high walls of the old city in the distance.

Tourists streamed into the port city every day, some heading for the cheap resorts packed with holiday-makers drinking and partying. But it also attracted the rich, who stayed in the city itself, or traveled out to luxury *fincas*, Moorish-style villas that dotted the island.

Morgan and Martin left the airport and hailed a taxi into Palma. It wound through the streets of the old city, the driver edging between closely packed stone walls, finally pulling up at the end of an alleyway. He pointed around the corner, indicating that it was too narrow for cars and they needed to walk the rest of the way.

Leaving their bags at the hotel, Morgan and Martin set off to explore the old city. The temperature was balmy, the sun harsh in direct light but they walked under the shade of cypress and palm trees through the sleepy streets. The sound of water drew them onward, and soon they emerged onto a promenade with sunken ponds and fountains in the Moorish style overhung with trees. The atmosphere was so different to Madrid. The bustling capital was all about rushing around achieving great things, but here the sense was only of languid relaxation.

"We should probably start at the cathedral," Martin said. "They have historic objects related to the early missions."

The promenade curved around in front of the Royal Palace of La Almudaina and up to the Carrer del Mirador, an open courtyard in front of the southern wall of the cathedral with a view out across the ocean toward North Africa.

Morgan looked up at the magnificent Gothic cathedral with its sandstone walls and flying buttresses that rose into the stark blue sky. Spain had a palpable sense of history and ancient faith that lived and breathed in its monuments. Even after living in Israel so long, Morgan felt that somehow Spain enmeshed itself more deeply into Catholicism, far more than the Holy Land ever could with its complication of triple faiths.

They walked around to the northern side and entered the main nave through a series of archways.

"I'll go find the archivist." Martin hurried away, barely restraining his enthusiasm for the quest.

Morgan remained in the nave, surprised to find that, despite its size, Palma Cathedral was warm and inviting. It was almost diametrically opposed to the dark chill of the cathedral in Toledo that had almost physically repelled her. This place felt alive, full of vibrant worshippers and tourists with broad smiles on their ruddy faces.

Perhaps it was the difference between the cities of Palma and Toledo themselves, one on the Mediterranean Sea, open to cultures sailing in from North Africa and other islands. Whereas Toledo shrunk inward, protecting itself, surrounded by high walls, Catholic doctrine and academic reasoning, shutting out those who might try to enter. Both were walled cities, but Palma felt welcoming, its walls more decorative than functional.

The cathedral was in the Levantine Gothic style with one of the largest rose windows in the world, known as the Gothic Eye. Arches supported the coffered ceiling, with different shades of stone and brick blending with dappled light streaming in through stained glass above.

Morgan sat down on a wooden pew at the back of the church looking down the nave toward the dramatic main altar. The architect Antoni Gaudí had adapted the cathedral at the start of the twentieth century, bringing an edge of modernism into the Gothic space. He created an ornate *baldachin*, a canopy over the altar in the shape of a crown of thorns. It was intricately designed with twisted wrought iron and glass panels in shades of amber and sunflowers, decorated with reeds of gold that sprouted toward heaven. Lights hung down from the edges in their own little canopies, and from afar, the *baldachin* looked weightless, suspended in space like a crown of gold as the crucified Savior hung on a colorful cross above.

Some hated Gaudí's modern take on religion, but Morgan remembered visiting the architect's still-unfinished masterpiece in Barcelona, the Sagrada Familia. That day she and Jake had tried to figure out Gaudí's numerical puzzle before the explosion that had begun the race to the Gates of Hell. That seemed so long ago now, and yet here she was in Spain again, on the trail of a Christian relic once more.

But this time without Jake.

As much as she enjoyed spending time with Martin, ARKANE's brilliant librarian was no field agent. Morgan thought of the Latino man and his team who followed in their footsteps, and the relic of the finger bone in her bag. She wouldn't be able to keep Martin safe as long as they had it with them.

She shifted on the pew as her burns itched, pain lancing through her as they rubbed against her jeans. For so long she had taken her body for granted, trusting her ability to fight her way out of trouble. But now she felt the weakness these injuries gave her, sapping her physical and emotional strength. Perhaps she couldn't keep Martin safe anyway right now.

Morgan sighed and leaned into the pain, pulling herself upright. She walked around the edge of the nave, past the chapels, trying to distract herself. At the Capella de Sant Benet, she looked up at the ornate altar with its golden columns and life-size statues of saints. At first glance, it looked similar to all the others – another martyr, another over-the-top shrine. But then she looked up and stopped in surprise, putting her face against the metal bars to see inside the sanctuary more closely.

A life-size skeleton climbed the wall of the chapel, its wings stretched out behind. Of course, there were often skeletons in these cathedrals, but Morgan had never seen a winged one. This was an unusual place indeed.

"There you are." Martin's voice startled her and Morgan turned around quickly. "Are you alright? You look like you've seen a ghost."

Morgan shook her head. "I'm just surprised by this place. It's … interesting."

"We'll have to explore it another time. I spoke to the archivist. He said the records of the missionaries are not here but in the church of the Franciscans a little way on through the city."

As they left the cathedral, Morgan glanced back at its high walls. She knew that she would come back here. The city felt so welcoming, and part of her simply wanted to sit at one of the cafés on the front overlooking the ocean with a gin and tonic enjoying the view and the sun on her face. But Martin walked swiftly on, fixed on their goal, determined to solve the puzzle of where the next relic might be.

It was only a ten-minute walk to the Plaça de Sant Francesc, and as they rounded the corner, Morgan spotted a larger-than-life statue of a friar in front of another massive church. The monk held a cross high with one hand, the other rested on the shoulder of a Mexican boy wearing a loin-cloth. They walked to the sign in front of it.

"Junípero Serra," Martin read. "Could this be the man we're looking for?"

Morgan examined the historic plaque. "He was born in the interior of the island, studied here in Palma and then went to New Mexico as a missionary, before founding the missions up the west coast of what became the USA." She looked up at Martin. "I'd say he's a prime candidate. Let's go inside and see what else we can find."

In any other city, where there were not so many monuments, this church would have been full of tourists. But Morgan and Martin were the only people in the ornate thirteenth-century church of Sant Francesc de Palma.

It was large, as big as any provincial cathedral, with niche chapels around the sides and an altar display of brilliant gold that shone in the sunlight streaming in from stained glass windows.

Morgan spotted a picture of Junípero Serra holding a crucifix as he preached to natives in the New World, next to a menorah and a replica Ark of the Covenant with angels on top, their outstretched wings protecting the tablet of the Ten Commandments within.

A darkened niche beyond contained a glass coffin with a full-size body inside. The crucified Jesus lay on a bloody shroud, the crown of thorns on his head, his face pallid and ashen, frozen in the agony of death. Morgan shuddered as she looked at it, the wax figure somehow more disturbing than the tortured saints around her.

"Look over here." Martin pointed out a sign commemorating a powerful sermon given by Junípero Serra in 1749 in honor of the blessed Ramon Llul. "Ramon was a medieval mystic, a wise man of the Franciscan order. His sepulcher is here. But more interesting is the fact that Junípero Serra preached here before he went to New Mexico."

"How do we know that he was the one who hid the finger bone?"

Martin smiled in triumph. "The text of his speech is printed here. He uses the metaphor of the Valley of Dry Bones to illuminate the need to spread the gospel to the New World. It must be him." He pointed to a map beside the printed text. "It also says that the relic of Serra himself is in San Francisco."

Morgan's heart sank a little at his words. Part of her wanted to continue the search, and now it seemed that she could just hand what they found back to Jake and Naomi in America. There was no reason for her to be involved in the search any longer. Martin would be relieved to go back to ARKANE HQ in London, and she could continue her Spanish holiday. Maybe even stay in Majorca, explore the island, drink that gin and tonic she'd been dreaming about before. It would be idyllic, relaxing.

Totally not what she wanted to do right now.

The mysterious relic had piqued her curiosity, the glimpse of the rugged Latino man gave her a sense of danger, and even the pain of her burns seemed to lessen while her mind was distracted by the mission.

Morgan shook her head, smiling at herself. She was an ARKANE agent, through and through. She just hoped that Director Marietti would allow her back and that Jake hadn't found himself a new partner in the meantime.

She looked at her watch, wondering what he was doing right now on the other side of the Atlantic.

CHAPTER 14

Louisiana bayou, USA.

NAOMI GASPED, A SHARP intake of breath. Her hands clutched tightly around her paddle, and she froze, even as the gentle current carried her closer to the alligator.

Fabienne paddled gently forward, barely touching the water, angling toward the bank.

"Stay over this side," she called softly. "They're used to the tourist air boats feeding them, but they don't usually bother kayakers."

Jake pulled his kayak up next to Naomi. Her eyes were wide with fear, fixed on the approaching alligator. She was breathing fast.

"It's OK," he said. "It's just curious."

The alligator swam closer and bumped against Naomi's kayak. She let out a small cry.

Then she made a break for it, paddling frantically for the closest island, her eyes fixed on the safe haven of the shore.

"Stop!" Jake reached for her kayak, his fingertips brushing the side, failing to get a hold of her.

The splashing drew the creature on, each stroke of its tail pushing it closer to her. Jake saw the full length of it as the weed parted, eight feet of powerful muscle with jaws that could rip a man in two. It could easily reach Naomi if it chose to, but it was still just curious. Orange plastic was not prey, but if the tasty flesh inside were to come close to its jaws ...

Jake couldn't wait any longer. He splashed the surface with his paddle, banging it down, moving it through the water in the likeness of a dying animal.

The alligator slowed and changed direction, slipping through the water back toward him.

Naomi reached the shore, making panicked noises as she tried to get out of the kayak.

"Stay inside," Fabienne shouted, paddling toward her. "The gators are fast on land, not just in the water."

Naomi didn't hear the words. Her eyes were huge, wide with the fixed stare of terror. Jake knew it well – narrowing vision, sound as if underwater, shallow breathing, the pounding of a fast heartbeat. The sense of near collapse. Naomi could not hear Fabienne's warnings. She was trapped in her own nightmare.

He banged his paddle down again.

Naomi put a hand out onto the bank to steady herself, but she found only swampland beneath. She tipped out into the shallows, splashing in the water, covered in stinking weed as she frantically tried to pull herself out onto the land.

The sound of her struggles drew the alligator's attention. It swerved away from Jake back to the shoreline, this time thrashing its tail and covering the distance incredibly fast.

Fabienne paddled swiftly toward the bank as the alligator crawled out of the water, its short legs hefting its huge body forward as its head swiveled to fix on its prey. Teeth poked out from powerful jaws, yellow with age, thick and sharp. Its tail thrashed from side to side as it stalked forward.

Naomi backed away, never taking her eyes from it, her fingers reaching behind her until she came up against a cypress tree.

The alligator closed in.

Fabienne paddled to the bank and pulled a chicken wing from her cooler bag. She threw it in front and to the side of the beast, the smell of meat turning its head away from Naomi. It snapped up the carcass.

Fabienne threw another chicken wing. "Over here, you big bully."

This time the meat landed in the shallows. The alligator turned its body to face the easy meal and snapped up the next morsel.

Naomi inched around the opposite side of the tree, moving almost imperceptibly. Fabienne kept throwing the wings as she paddled slowly backwards, drawing the alligator back into the water.

"Help her with the kayak," she called to Jake. "Meet me on the other side of this island. I'll draw him away. Guess we'll have to eat something else at Grandma's."

As Fabienne disappeared around the corner of the channel, a chicken-laden Pied Piper of the bayou, Jake paddled over to the shoreline.

Now the alligator was out of sight, Naomi sank down to the ground, her head in her hands. Her clothes were soaked with swamp water and dotted with duckweed.

"I'm so sorry." Her voice cracked with tears. "I don't know what I was doing."

"It's OK, I know those things can be terrifying. Remind me to tell you about the crocs I encountered in the Tugela River in KwaZulu-Natal sometime." Jake held her kayak with a firm hand. "Now get back in, and let's go find Albertine and get you into some dry clothes."

Naomi eased herself back into the kayak and together they paddled around the side of the island in the opposite direction to Fabienne. As the minutes passed, Jake wondered if they would be left alone to fend for themselves for the night – but then they heard the soft dip of a paddle in the water.

Fabienne emerged from the side of the island. "Right, let's hurry now, before he finishes that batch of chicken."

She led the way further into the depths of the bayou.

It wasn't long before they rounded a bend and the waterway opened up into a creek. A ramshackle wooden hut sat on stilts over the water, its timbers speckled green with lichen. Albertine sat on the deck smoking a cigarette, looking out to the shadows. A flock of tiny birds darted above and around her, picking insects from the air even as the atmosphere thickened with approaching rain.

The old woman raised a hand at their approach, no trace of surprise on her face. She had known they would come. She nodded at Jake as if everything were proceeding exactly as planned, as if everything moved with the surety of the slow-moving waters of the bayou. Their two rivers would meet and merge for a time, then separate again. He wondered what else she knew.

They paddled the kayaks to the water's edge and tied them to a jetty of weathered wooden planks covered in slippery algae. Fabienne helped Naomi out.

"You can change into dry clothes in the hut. It's better on the inside. Come on, I'll show you."

The two women walked off to the hut, while Jake pulled the kayaks further up the bank. He walked over to Albertine and sat next to her on the deck. Neither spoke as the sounds of the bayou washed over them – the croak of bullfrogs, the call of night-birds, the rustle of hunted creatures in the reeds beneath.

Albertine took another drag of her cigarette, exhaling smoke into the air around them. "I knew you'd come. A white man took the bones from Africa, and a white man must now pay the price. That's how the story goes. When the ground shifted at St Louis, and the bone chamber revealed, I knew it was finally time." She looked down at Jake. "Then you came."

Fabienne stepped out from the hut, shaking her head in frustration at the words. "Grandma, you know how I feel about those myths. They hold our community back. Keep us stuck in the old ways."

Albertine smiled, her old face full of love as she looked at her granddaughter.

"They're not myths, child. The bones are real, our faith is real, and the *loa* say that the time is now upon us."

Naomi came outside wearing dry clothes and joined them on the deck. Jake was relieved to see her looking much happier now they were off the water. Her eyes were bright and inquisitive as she sat down next to Albertine.

"What do you know about the bone chamber?"

Albertine shrugged. "I've never seen it, but the Hand of Ezekiel was split between the nations, not buried in that tomb. There are five fingers, each needed to complete the relic. And I know they weren't all down there." She gave a mischievous smile. "Because we have one."

Jake thought of the picture Morgan had sent from Spain, the finger bone from the Toledo reliquary. Could there really be five of them? And if so, was the second one within reach?

Albertine continued. "The secret of the relic has been kept in the voodoo community since the time of Marie Laveau. The priest Père Antoine gave it to her to hide from those in the Catholic Church who wished to use its power once more. His Brotherhood had been infiltrated, so he told her to hide it until the time came when the bone chamber revealed itself."

She reached down and gripped Jake's shoulder. Her touch was light, but he could feel a wiry strength in her, and more than that, a sense that she knew of what he had been through because she too had seen beyond the human realm.

"But first, *cher*, you must prove yourself worthy."

"How?" Jake asked.

Albertine was silent as she took another drag on her cigarette and blew the smoke into the heavy air.

"The relic belongs to the one who rises from the dead."

Jake raised an eyebrow, the corkscrew scar twisting away. "That's a tall order."

Albertine cackled with laughter. "It's a ritual, and if you survive, the relic is yours." She pointed at a shovel that lay against the side of the hut. "First, you must dig your own grave."

CHAPTER 15

Albertine's words hung in the air like the breath of nightshade. Jake considered them as he looked at the shovel and beyond to a patch of more level ground higher on the bank.

"That's crazy," Naomi said. "Why would he dig his own grave?"

Albertine shrugged. "It's a choice. We can have some dinner, enjoy the peace. You can sleep here and go in the morning." She looked at Jake. "Without the relic. Or you can endure the ritual and – if you survive – leave with the finger bone."

Jake stood up. The timbers of the deck creaked as he walked to the shovel, hefted its weight in his hand.

He walked up the bank and began to dig. The ground had been softened by rain, and as Jake thrust the blade into the fertile earth, he cut through worms in the dirt, slicing them into pieces, leaving their wriggling bodies behind. He shoveled the soil to one side then swung again.

Naomi came up to join him, her arms wrapped around herself for comfort, a barrier against the encroaching dark.

"Are you really going through with this ritual? We don't even know what it is. She might not even have the relic."

Her jaw was tight, a deep frown between her brows.

Jake kept digging. "I believe Albertine has it, and this is her price. You're a researcher. Don't you want to know what might happen? After all, few outsiders ever see a real voodoo rite."

Jake had heard of ritual resurrection ceremonies back in South Africa. Some of those who entered never made it through to the other side, but those who did, came back transformed. He had always lived on the boundary of the supernatural and perhaps he strayed too far over that edge sometimes. But he craved the moments beyond the veil.

And he wanted that relic.

A slow drumbeat came from the deck. Albertine stood over the water, her back straight, as she thumped the drum with a soulful rhythm. The deep tone echoed across the bayou, traveling across the dark water.

"She's calling to others." Naomi shivered. "I'm worried, Jake. What if this goes wrong?"

He reached out a hand to take hers. "You'd better pull me out of this grave if it looks like I'm actually dying." He grinned. "But seriously, this is a ritual, not a murder. The point is to emerge on the other side."

* * *

As Jake squeezed her hand, Naomi heard the confidence in his words, an edge of anticipation, the almost visceral need that he had to go through this ritual. But she couldn't help the dread that rose up at the thought of what could happen.

Her mama had told stories of what slaves had gone through in the days when white men ruled them with whips and chains and fire. Voodoo was born from the blood of those ripped from their home to die here in a foreign land, and Jake could never understand that, even with his African heritage.

But he was an experienced ARKANE agent, and Naomi had heard stories of what he had faced on other missions – demons from hell, mythical creatures, artifacts of great power. Surely he knew what he was doing?

"It'll be fine, I promise." Jake dropped her hand and returned to digging.

Naomi stood watching him for a moment, the muscles in his back straining as he lifted the heavy earth. She was still ashamed by what had happened in the bayou, and perhaps the residual fear made her worry more than she should. The jaws of the alligator had come so close, and she could almost feel its jagged teeth biting into her flesh with crushing pain. Naomi pushed the thought away. Sometimes her imagination was a liability, and if she was going to make it as a field agent, she needed to put aside the stories of her childhood. Jake was the senior agent on this case, and she had to trust that he would get them through this.

The door of the hut creaked, and Naomi turned at the sound. Fabienne walked out, her arms laden with firewood. Her shoulders were still stiff, and there was a petulant set to her mouth, but she seemed resigned to her grandmother's plan. She set the logs down and began to build a fire in a pit surrounded by stones a few meters away. Naomi went to help her, turning away from Jake, leaving him to his own thoughts.

* * *

Jake continued to dig, making sure the grave was long and wide enough for his frame, while still shallow enough to get out of. He was sweating with the effort, but he still felt a chill. The hairs on the back of his neck prickled and his heart beat out of time. His breath caught in his throat and panic rose as he finished the grave.

What in hell was he thinking? This was crazy.

Jake looked up at the stars, bright in the night sky above now they were away from the city. The smell of wood smoke filled the air, drifting through the bayou. Bullfrogs croaked, and the slow beat of Albertine's drum marked the passing of time, counting down the minutes until he would lie in the cool earth. Jake took a deep breath, inhaling slowly and then exhaling for a count of four.

He thought of Morgan, half a world away in Spain, wished she was here with him. He smiled as he considered that she would probably want to be the one in the grave experiencing the edge of the unknown. But he would have made sure she came back.

Jake looked over at Naomi by the fire. She was a good agent in many ways, but this mission was turning into way more than she could handle. They had grown closer in New York, and she had emerged a lot stronger after that mission, but she had little experience in the field. He looked down at the grave. There was no going back now. He had to take his chances.

The drumbeat changed as lights appeared on the bayou, lanterns on the front of kayaks moving through the water-ways as the voodoo community arrived for the ritual. The sound of paddles dipping into water joined the drum, then the first notes of a song filled the air. A slave hymn from the Deep South. A song of pain and suffering, of a people beaten down and yet still they would rise.

Jake closed his eyes. The music stirred something within him that he hadn't felt in a long time. His skin was not black, but he was proudly African, and he felt the pulse of the old country in the refrain, a stirring of home. Jake straddled both worlds, and if he were to die here tonight, his body would be part of this ancient place and lie alongside these people.

Not such a bad way to go.

The new arrivals pulled their kayaks high up on the banks

as the drumbeat picked up its pace, songs blending together as more people arrived, joining their voices to the chorus.

They gathered around the fire, flames flickering over their features. Jake noticed people of all kinds amongst them. Old and wrinkled, wise beyond years. Young and beautiful, ready for the heightened experience of the *loa* possession. A Creole woman looked over and met his gaze. She had unusual sapphire eyes, and the firelight glinted off brilliant blue beads in her hair, her sculptured features like a goddess from another age.

Albertine gave the drum to an older man by the fire, and he continued with the rhythmic beat. She shuffled over to Jake and offered him a glass bottle filled with a brown liquid.

"Drink. The *loa* come when your guard is down. This will help."

Jake took the bottle from her. There was no label, no indication of what was inside. It smelled of something herbal and a hint of fallen leaves, the edge of seasons turning, that moment when summer fades and decay sets in.

He lifted it to his lips and drank deep. The liquid burned on the way down with the fire of spirit and snaked its way into his blood. The rush of alcohol made his head spin, and as Jake gazed into the fire beyond, he saw misshapen figures dancing there, twitching to the beat of the drum.

Albertine followed his gaze and nodded. "For some, the ritual is life-giving. For others it is poison, and there is no cure." She reached for his hand. "You must go willingly to the grave. Do you accept?"

Jake took another swig from the bottle, allowing the sensation of floating to ease through his body. He rarely ever let go like this, preferring to stay in control, always watching for threat, always ready to fight. But he saw something he desperately wanted in Albertine's eyes. An acceptance of this dual world. An understanding that good and evil were married together, each a different form of truth.

"I accept."

Albertine smiled. "Then we begin."

She signaled to the man playing the drum, and he shifted the beat, using both hands to create a rhythm that sliced through the night, calling out over dark waters to that which lay curled beneath.

Albertine etched *veve*, voodoo designs, on the earth that would act as a beacon for the *loa*. She poured out some of the liquid from the bottle onto the ground, chanting as the drum beat faster.

Jake's heart throbbed in time, the deep resonance vibrating through him down into the earth.

Fat raindrops fell as the storm broke overhead. Jake looked up to see a vortex of dark cloud whirling above and in the shadows, he saw silhouettes of huge wings. He blinked, and they were gone, leaving only the rain. It washed over him, soaking through his clothes, turning the earth to mud at his feet.

Albertine began to dance, other women joining her as they chanted and called for the *loa* to descend. With one foot firmly rooted to the earth, the old woman turned around, shaking arms held to the sky. The rain poured down, soaking her, but still she whirled, calling to the spirits in guttural tones that seemed to come from the depths of her soul.

As the *loa* descended, Albertine began to shake. Convulsions wracked her whole body as the spirits took hold. She whirled and danced and stomped and cried out.

Then suddenly she stopped. The drums fell silent.

She pointed at Jake. "Now, you die."

Her voice was different, more masculine, deeper somehow. Jake felt an energy push against his chest as the old woman held her hand out toward him.

Those around forced Jake to his knees in front of the grave. The cold wet mud soaked through to his skin, the smell of rich soil flooding his senses. In that final moment, he still had a choice. Tendrils of the drugged potion tugged at his mind, drawing him toward the shadow, but he still had the strength to resist. He could push these people off, take Naomi away from here, forget the relic. The worshippers would not follow them.

But Jake wanted this.

Perhaps his whole life was a search for the boundary of what was real. He was so close to the edge this time. Perhaps he would tip over it. He had to take that chance.

He stretched out in the grave, face up, looking at the bright stars above as those around him began to shovel earth over his body from his feet up.

Jake's heart pounded as the cool earth landed, the sensation heavy over his legs, rising up his body, pinning him down. He clenched his fists, trying not to react, trying to resist the rising panic at the sensation of crushing earth.

This was a ritual, a mirror of death, not death itself. Surely they would stop soon?

But as they filled in the earth over his chest, Jake realized that he couldn't move anymore. His limbs were heavy from the drugged spirit, and the soil held him firm in the grave. In a moment of clarity, he looked at those around him, no longer seeing rational humans, but believers possessed by the *loa*.

They were going to bury him alive.

This would be his grave.

Jake wriggled in the earth-bound tomb. "No more. Stop!"

A shovelful of dirt came down on his face, filling his mouth with rich earth and pieces of still-wriggling worms. He spat, shaking his head as more earth cascaded down his neck. He strained to escape, but he was buried under too much heavy soil. He couldn't get up.

* * *

Naomi couldn't stand to watch anymore. Jake was going to die under that dirt in this god-forsaken place of nightmares unless she got him out of there.

"Stop! Let him up."

She reached for him, crawling forward, arms outstretched, shouting at those around her to help.

Strong arms pulled her back, held her down, and Naomi looked up into faces with blank eyes possessed by the *loa*, uncaring of what might happen to the white man in the pit. A flash of blue beads and then a woman knelt beside her, bottle in her hand.

"Drink this, *cher*. All is as it should be."

"No, I have to –" Naomi's words were cut off as the woman forced her head back, pinched her nose and poured the fiery liquid down her throat. She couldn't help but gulp it down even as she fought back. As the flames rose higher, the chanting louder, Naomi felt the edges of reality soften and fade to black.

* * *

As another shovel of dirt fell upon his face, Jake could only watch as the Creole woman with brilliant blue beads in her hair dragged Naomi into the shadows outside the edge of the fire.

He tried to call for her, but dirt filled his mouth.

He coughed, choking on the stink of the swamp. Jake snatched a final breath as earth covered his face and everything went black.

His heart pounded as he lay in the grave.

It was as if he felt every grain of dirt against his skin, as if he could smell the creatures who had died in this earth, as if he could see through the veil. An opening into the vast universe, a glimpse beyond the edge of what was truly real.

As he held his breath, Jake thought of all he had seen with ARKANE, of all he had experienced of life beyond the visible. In that moment, he called to the God of his childhood. He called to the angel bound in chains. He even called to the demon of the bone church who had left its mark on his skin.

And as the final breath in his lungs was crushed from his body, Jake called for Morgan.

CHAPTER 16

Palma, Majorca, Spain.

MORGAN WOKE WITH A start.

"Jake!" His name flew from her lips as she felt the spark of his life go out. Her skin was slick with sweat, her breath ragged as she surfaced from the nightmare.

Sunlight filtered in through the curtains and Morgan shook her head, trying to remember what she had seen. Dark shadows, flickering flames, the dead weight of earth shoveled onto a prone body.

She reached for her phone. No messages from Jake.

It was the early hours of the morning in New Orleans. He was probably asleep. She wouldn't ring him now. Better to wait until later when she could ask him what to do about San Francisco. After the red-eye flight, she had needed a nap and now felt at least partially renewed.

Morgan rolled out of bed, turned on the coffee machine, and walked naked into the bathroom, catching sight of herself in the mirror. The wound dressings on her burned legs were a putrid yellow, the injuries still seeping pus and blood. The dull ache of constant pain was a background note to her every waking hour. The scar on her side stood out as a pale slash against her olive skin, and she could count her ribs. She had lost weight and muscle tone in the recovery process while her mind had been lost in doubt and fear.

Losing Father Ben had been one sacrifice too far, but Dinah was right. Ben had chosen his path many years before Morgan had even been born. He had lived his life fighting for the side of light, and she would honor him by doing the same.

Besides, what else was she going to do now? Return to the university or work in a psychology practice? After everything she had seen, she couldn't go back to that mundane life.

If she wanted to work alongside Jake again, she needed to put the past behind her. These injuries would fade, but it was her mind that needed to be strong. It was time to get back in the game.

* * *

Louisiana bayou, USA.

Jake leaned into death, his mind soaring with the expanse of the universe. The light beckoned, and he embraced it, letting everything else fall away. His parents were in the light, his sisters, all those he had lost, and now he would be with them. He reached out and his fingertips brushed against his mother's hand. She smiled, her lips forming his name. A great joy filled his soul –

Then, wrenching pain.

He was ripped away. The soil brushed from his face, his mouth wiped clean. Many hands removed rocks and earth from his body and pulled him from the grave.

Jake knelt on all fours as he retched up muddy earth. He gasped for breath, coughing, spluttering, holding onto that last moment of the light. A sense of desolation filled him as it blinked out and he bit back tears. His family had been taken years ago, butchered at their ranch in South Africa. Now he had lost them again.

He brushed the dirt from his eyes and opened them.

The sounds of the bayou returned. A log shifted in the fire, and the crackle of the flames brought him back to the present.

Albertine crouched in front of him, her eyes human again, the *loa* quiet until next time.

"You have been born-again from the earth. Your bones are resurrected. You have passed through." She pulled a small walnut-wood box from her pocket, carved with the intricate whorls of the wind, and handed it to him.

Jake took the box and opened it carefully. A fat finger bone with a stopper of red wax lay on a bed of faded yellow ribbon.

Albertine put her hand on his. "This is one of the fingers from the Hand of Ezekiel. It is yours now, Jake. My ancestors protected it for generations. Do not let it resurrect those who should stay in the grave."

Jake nodded. "I'll protect it. I'll honor their memory."

At his words, the people around them began to fade into the shadows, heading for their kayaks, leaving the ritual ground for their homes and a new day ahead.

As the crowd cleared, Jake looked around, suddenly frantic. "Where's Naomi?" He stood up. "There was a woman with blue beads in her hair holding Naomi back from the grave. Where is she? Who is she?"

Albertine's face creased in concern. "Lashonda Milton. She's a new member of the voodoo community, but I knew her mama when she was alive. She's a good girl, *cher*. There must be some explanation."

"We need to find her." Jake ran to the end of the deck, scanning the bayou. "Naomi!" he called out over the water, hearing only the sound of bullfrogs in return. He spun around. "We could still find them. They can't have gone far."

Albertine came to stand by him, looking out into the darkness. "They could have gone in many directions. Lashonda knows the bayou. She will have planned a way out."

The sound of an engine pierced the still night, a motorboat beyond the island.

Jake started for his kayak, but Fabienne grabbed his arm. "We won't make it in time. They'll be gone by the time we paddle out there. But she lives in the city, works there too. I'll guide you. You'll never make it back alone."

"Maybe we can track them." Jake raced back to the hut, digging through the bags until he found his cell phone. "Damn it. No signal."

His mind whirled as he considered what to do next. This was his fault. He should have listened to Naomi's fear, her intuition that this would go wrong. He put his hand in his pocket and pulled out the box with the relic inside. He hoped it was worth the price.

Albertine hobbled over. "There are many who seek the Hand of Ezekiel." Her face suddenly looked much older, the wrinkles on her skin deepening with the shadows of night. "The bones of the dead for the life of the living. That may be your choice now." She shook her head. "The relic has always been a curse. I'm glad to be rid of it, but I'm sorry to pass it on to you."

Jake cupped her hands in his and looked down into her dark eyes. "You've done all you could. You and your family protected the relic for generations. I'll do my best to keep it from those who would use it for evil, but I have to get Naomi back."

He bent and kissed the old woman on the cheek, knowing that now their rivers parted ways and that hers would soon flow beyond the veil. "Goodbye, Albertine."

Fabienne kissed her grandmother, then she and Jake

packed up the kayaks quickly, launching them into the dark waters. A fleeting thought of alligators feeding on Naomi's broken body flashed through Jake's mind, but he pushed it aside, gritting his teeth for the journey ahead. She would be safe as long as he had the relic.

Without Naomi to slow them down, Jake and Fabienne paddled hard, making good time back to the wharf. They stowed the kayaks and jogged back to the car where Jake finally got a signal on his phone.

He dialed Martin Klein. "Things have gone south here. Naomi's been taken."

"Oh, my goodness." Martin's voice wavered with concern. "I can track her phone. Just a minute."

"She was taken from the bayou south of New Orleans." Jake looked at his watch. "Two hours ago now, so she can't have gone too far. I also need you to see if you can find a woman called Lashonda Milton. She has blue beads in her hair. I saw her with Naomi before …"

"Before what?" Martin asked.

"It doesn't matter now." Jake shook his head, the events of earlier that night more like a dream that had swiftly turned into a nightmare.

"Morgan's probably up by now," Martin said. "You want me to go next door and let her know what's going on?"

"No. I'll call her myself."

Jake hung up then dialed again, the phone ringing once, twice. "Come on. Pick up." He willed Morgan to answer.

"Jake?"

Her voice was sweet relief, and Jake felt a glimmer of hope that somehow this might work out.

"Naomi's been taken. I need your help."

"What do you mean, she's been taken? By who?"

Jake shook his head. "I'm not sure as yet, but it has to be related to the relics. I've got one here that matches the finger bone that you and Martin found."

"What can I do?"

Jake walked further away from the car, leaving Fabienne behind so she couldn't hear what he was saying.

"I know you needed a break after Israel and you helped with the Toledo relic because I asked you to, because you were already there. But I need your help, Morgan." Jake paused. "I need my partner back. We lost Ben, and I can't let that happen again. We can't lose Naomi. She shouldn't have been out in the field on a mission like this. It's bigger than we thought."

Morgan's breathing came over the line. He could almost hear her thinking.

"It'll probably take me ten to twelve hours to get to New Orleans, maybe quicker if Martin can get me on a special flight."

"Pack your things. He's already tracing the woman I saw with Naomi before she was taken. There are so many things I need to tell you. Things I saw last night, things that you would believe and many others wouldn't."

Morgan laughed softly. Jake closed his eyes and let the welcome sound wash over him. "We've certainly seen a few things together. Hang in there Jake, I'm coming."

* * *

Charity Hospital, New Orleans, USA.

Luis looked down at the young woman who lay shackled to the hospital bed in one of the private rooms. She was still under the influence of the drugged liquid, and she moaned in her sleep, writhing on the bed as if she was trying to escape something chasing her from the shadows.

"I saw the relic, one of the finger bones," Lashonda said as she paced up and down. She cupped her hands together as if holding the precious object. "It was right there, but I couldn't take it. This was the only way." She came closer to the bed and bent over Naomi. "I think I gave her too much though. She should be out of it by now."

"She'll come round." Luis reached out a hand and held Lashonda's arm. "And you're sure her partner has the relic now?"

"Yes, but I don't think he understands its true power. I saw them speak together. He cares for her." Lashonda pulled out her smart phone. "As the *loa* descended, I stood at the back. This is the man before they buried him."

Luis took the phone and looked at the image, his eyes examining the muscular figure. The man was rugged, physically strong, but there was something else compelling about him. He clearly understood life beyond the physical or the voodoo believers wouldn't have welcomed him into their midst.

"They really buried him?"

Lashonda nodded. "I left with Naomi as they shoveled the last of the dirt onto his face, but before we left on the motorboat, I heard the celebration as he rose again. He will have the relic now."

Luis swiped at the screen, loading the image to a recognition database. As part of their almost unlimited funding, the clinic had access to government records. It was only seconds before matching pictures of the man came up on screen.

Jake Timber, ARKANE agent.

Responsible for countless missions tracking down religious relics and ancient artifacts around the world.

Number of verified kills: 23.

There were many pages of accompanying notes, but Luis skipped over them and clicked on *Known Associates.*

The woman who lay in front of them came up. Naomi Locasto, linguist at ARKANE's New York office. And then, Morgan Sierra, her face matching the picture from the Toledo synagogue security footage.

Luis smiled as a plan began to form in his mind. He looked down at Naomi, placed a hand on her cheek, then trailed his fingers down to her neck, circling her throat.

Naomi's phone rang. The screen flashed with a name: *Jake.*

Luis picked up the phone and answered it.

"What have you done with her, you bastard?" Jake had a faint South African accent, his anger palpable through the line.

"She's safe. For now."

"Who are you? What do you want?"

Luis tightened his grip a little around Naomi's flesh. She moaned in her sleep, tried to clutch at her neck, but the shackles prevented her. They rattled against the bars of the bed.

"What's that sound? Are you hurting her?"

Luis relaxed his grip, stroked the soft skin where he had left a faint mark. "She's unharmed, for now. But I want what you have in exchange for her. I want the Hand of Ezekiel. Bring me the two relics you already have along with the others, and you can have her back."

There was silence for a moment, then Jake's voice came again, hesitant, questioning. "What you mean – the others?"

Luis bent closer to the phone. "I know of the Toledo relic, and there are three more along with the one you were given last night. The Hand of Ezekiel is made up of five finger bones. You will bring me them all."

"We have two of the pieces, but I don't know where the others are. I have no way of finding out any time soon."

Luis pulled up images of the bone box on the phone. "I'll send you a map. It's rough, but it gives some indication of where the other relics are. Peru, the Philippines, and San Francisco, where I'll meet you on the third day. I'll send instructions later. Bring all the relics with you or Naomi will go through the same ritual you did – but with nobody to pull her from the dirt."

Luis hung up the phone as Jake began to shout words that needed no translation.

CHAPTER 17

Louisiana bayou, USA.

JAKE LOOKED OUT AT the live oak trees, the frown deepening between his eyebrows. The Spanish moss had a sinister look now, as if the lacy web choked the life from its host. Leaves rustled in the breeze, and the dawn chorus of birdsong began, a reminder that the world continued to turn whatever happened next. Martin could track Naomi's phone. They could find out who had her, get her back, but would that be enough?

He pulled the wooden box from his pocket and opened it to look at the relic. The finger bone was a sickly yellow as if it had been kept in a smoky room for generations, the wax stopper a thickened crimson. It seemed a paltry thing, but the vaults beneath ARKANE in London were filled with such objects. Many held tremendous power and had cost much to find and keep from those who would use them for evil. Jake had once doubted the power those artifacts held, but he had seen enough over his time with ARKANE to convince him that all myths had truth at their heart. If these relics could somehow raise the dead, then they belonged in the vault.

The man on the phone would keep Naomi safe until the

exchange in three days, which gave them time to figure out how to get her back *and* keep the relics.

His phone beeped.

A text from Naomi's number. Pictures of a box of bone inlaid with tiny rubies, its surface patterned with a map outlined in blood. Jake enlarged it, squinting at the lines. The scale made it hard to see, but one precious stone did indeed sit over the islands of the Philippines in the Western Pacific.

Jake forwarded it to Martin to narrow down possible locations. He called Morgan back.

"Change of plan. Don't come to New Orleans. We need to get the other three relics in the next three days and exchange the whole lot of them for Naomi."

"Tall order," Morgan said. "I hope you know where they are."

"One's in the Philippines. Another in Peru. The final one is in San Francisco, where we do the exchange."

The sound of footsteps as Morgan paced her room. "All places once ruled by the Spanish Empire. Makes sense but it's a pretty big area to search."

"Let's start with the Philippines – go the furthest distance first. By the time we both get there, Martin should have some leads."

"I'll see you in the Philippines then."

Jake smiled as Morgan ended the call. A glimmer of hope flickered into life. This mission hadn't turned out the way he'd expected, but he would soon have his partner back.

* * *

Charity Hospital, New Orleans, USA.

Naomi heard the rhythmic beep of monitors and smelled the heavy scent of lilies with an undertone of antiseptic as she swam into consciousness. Her eyelids were heavy but even with them closed, she sensed she was somewhere medical. She scanned her body for injuries, finding nothing but the sluggish aftermath of whatever she had been drugged with. Her mind flashed back to her last memory of the bayou.

Jake.

She opened her eyes and tried to sit up, held back by metal shackles around her wrists even as she took in her surroundings. A private medical suite with top-of-the-range equipment, white walls, a green curtain pulled around her.

The curtain swished as it was pulled back by an older man with the elegant features of a patrician Spaniard. He leaned on an ebony walking cane, his back twisted with some kind of congenital disease.

"Good. You're awake." The man's smile was friendly, but his eyes were hooded, like a snake mesmerizing its prey.

"Where am I? Where's Jake? How did I get here?"

The man held his hand up to stop her questions, his authority clear. Naomi fell silent, heart pounding as she realized she was a long way from any help.

"I'm Luis Rey, and this is my daughter, Elena." He stepped sideways, pulling the curtain further open to reveal a young girl in another hospital bed close by, her face pale and sick. Her fragile body twisted under the sheets with what looked like advanced stage of the same disease her father suffered. She moaned in her sleep, frowning in pain. Naomi's heart beat faster, seeing in the little girl a shadow of her lost sister, Esther.

Luis stepped forward and took his daughter's hand. "You're here to save her life."

* * *

Cebu City, Philippines.

Morgan walked out of the private airport terminal, looking around expectantly. Martin had managed to get her on a military transport from Spain, and she had spent the flight reading up on the spread of Catholicism under the Spanish Empire. She was desperate to discuss it all with Jake, but she couldn't see him. Her heart sank a little. She hefted her bag over one shoulder and walked toward the taxi ranks. He was probably waiting outside.

A group of tourists moved on behind their guide, and suddenly, he was there.

Jake stood at a coffee bar, reading a local paper. He had more than a few days' worth of dark stubble and his shirt was crumpled, but he held his athletic frame with readiness. Morgan knew how swiftly he could move if he needed to. Her heart beat a little faster, and she couldn't stop the smile that dawned at seeing him again.

He looked up, and his amber eyes caught hers. He smiled back across the crowded terminal, and they both walked toward each other, dodging the tourists and business commuters.

As they reached each other, Jake pulled Morgan into his arms. She leaned into his embrace, feeling the strong muscles in his back under her hands. She closed her eyes and for a moment, let his heart beat against hers. They stood for a second longer than friends would.

Then they pulled apart.

"Have you heard from Naomi?"

Jake shook his head. "Just a picture sent by her kidnapper to show that she's alive. Let's keep her that way. We only have a few days to find the relics."

Morgan grinned. "We've had worse odds."

Jake laughed but then looked at her more closely. Morgan was aware of the dark shadows beneath her eyes, the taut muscles in her jaw that the painkillers didn't quite relax.

"Are you OK to do this? It looks like you're limping. How are your burns?"

Morgan took a deep breath. "You remember how it felt after that ton of bones fell on you at the Sedlec ossuary?"

Jake shook his head. "I'll never forget it."

"It's a bit like that. Only a flesh wound." She grimaced a little. "Honestly, I want to be here, Jake. I want to be on this mission. Naomi might have been safe if I had come with you in the first place, so this is just as much my responsibility as it is yours."

They walked back to the coffee table, and Jake opened up a text.

"Martin tracked the phone. The man who has Naomi is Luis Rey, a billionaire whose wealth stems from the Spanish Empire, and now runs a lab spearheading immortality research, backed by the military – unofficially, of course." He gave a wry smile. "He also has a daughter who suffers from a congenital disease that Rey thinks the relic may cure. So, Marietti wants us to stay on mission. Given what's at stake, he's confident that Naomi will be safe until the exchange so we'll see how far we can get before then."

He pulled out a map of the Philippines. "Any thoughts on where to start looking?"

Morgan pointed at the Northern islands. "I've been reading Martin's research on the flight. The explorer Magellan claimed the Philippines for the King of Spain in 1521, when the Spanish began converting the locals and trading in the area. They ruled the Philippines for 333 years, and it's still predominantly Catholic. Many of the oldest churches are in Manila, but there are also Spanish settlements dotted around the islands in the central and south."

"So where should we start? We don't have much time, so we can't go north *and* south – unless we split up."

Jake looked at her, and she saw hesitation in his eyes. Now they were back together again, neither of them wanted to be apart so soon.

She shook her head. "That shouldn't be necessary. We just need to make a choice. Based on the relics so far, it seems most likely that the finger bones were carried by missionary friars. There's a place in Manila that fits the profile – Quiapo Church which holds the statue of the Black Nazarene."

Jake raised an eyebrow. "If that links Africa with Spain, then it fits with some of what I learned in the bayou."

His expression was troubled. Morgan reached for his hand. "Are you going to tell me what happened there?"

He took a deep breath. "I'm not really sure myself, to be honest. I'll save it for when we have time to reflect, but what about this Black Nazarene?"

Morgan brought out her smart phone and swiped to the pictures that Martin had provided. "It's one of the most popular objects of devotion in the Philippines. Millions come to the annual Traslación, the Savior's passage around the city."

Jake leaned in to look at the picture. "Funky outfit."

The kneeling Christ was clothed in a maroon velvet tunic embroidered in gold with lace around its neck and cuffs in the Spanish traditional style. A golden crown of thorns on his head supported three rays of light signifying his divinity. He knelt on a wooden platform, carrying his cross toward the crucifixion, eyes fixed on heaven above.

Morgan looked into the face of the Black Nazarene, puzzled anew by the Catholic obsession with physical representations of the divine. In the Jewish tradition of her father, God was unseeable, unknowable. Reducing him to this human condition weakened him. But perhaps that was what made the Savior more accessible to the downtrodden, to those who suffered every day in a country with some of the most densely populated cities on earth.

The statue's skin was not really black, more a burnished mahogany, his features carved with the care and devotion of a true believer.

"He's carved from mesquite wood and comes from Mexico or New Spain back in the days of Empire. The statue arrived in the Philippines in 1606 along with missionaries and traders."

Jake frowned. "That's too early, isn't it?"

Morgan nodded, then zoomed in on the photo. "But look at this, his fingers are missing and there are lines in some local histories that refer to relics replacing them over time."

Jake leaned back and took a sip of his coffee. "I don't know. It feels different from the ones we've found so far. The Brotherhood haven't flaunted any of the other relics. Quite the opposite, in fact. They've been hidden. But this Black Nazarene is so high profile. Any other options?"

Morgan bent to the map, tracing the thousands of islands that made up the Philippines as she examined the names. She stopped suddenly, her finger on a tiny land mass in the middle of the blue.

Jake smiled. "Now that looks more like it."

*　*　*

Camiguin, Philippines.

The tiny plane swooped over turquoise white-capped waves as it came down to land on the volcanic island of Camiguin. Morgan looked out the window, her forehead pressed against the glass as she gazed down at the idyllic paradise ringed by white sand beaches and offshore reefs with a mountainous interior of lush green forest.

It didn't seem like the kind of place to come searching for the dead, but Spanish explorers had settled here in 1598, building a watchtower that looked over the sea to keep an eye out for pirates. The settlement had been home for Spanish and locals alike for two hundred years before it had been destroyed by the birth of Mount Vulcan in 1871. A fissure opened up near the village of Catarman, destroying the town, and now the ruins of the Spanish church, bell tower and cemetery lay peacefully beneath the blue Bohol Sea.

Morgan turned to Jake seated next to her. "It's so beautiful. No wonder the Spanish settled here. Martin's research said that this is one of the oldest settlements and a Spanish Franciscan friar from the same college as Junípero Serra came to this island, a possible link to the Hand of Ezekiel."

Jake leaned over to get a better look. "It makes more sense that the relic was kept here, away from highly populated areas. What better place than a remote island?"

After landing, they hefted their packs off the plane and walked down the steps. It was hot and humid, definitely tropical, and Morgan took a deep breath, enjoying the balmy air on her skin and the scent of flowers on the sea breeze.

A young Filipino man stood waiting at the edge of the tarmac. He waved as they walked toward his Jeep, the back section loaded up with dive gear and spare tanks ready for their excursion to the sunken city.

"Welcome to the island born of fire. I'm Amado." His smile was wide with the good humor of the locals, famous for their welcome. "Get in, get in, we should dive before dusk falls."

Amado drove them along the main road around the island, past turnoffs for waterfalls and protected hiking areas. "There are many things to do here," he explained with enthusiasm. "I can show you once you've finished your dive. You can swim at our famous cascades with orchids and ferns, or perhaps you might like to see the famous Camiguin

Hanging Parrot or the hawk owl. We get many birdwatchers here. Or the hot springs. You can relax there with a glass of wine and look out over the ocean."

Jake groaned. "That sounds exactly what I want to do. If only we had the time."

Morgan looked over at him and wondered if she and Jake would ever get to spend time relaxing and drinking wine in a hot pool together.

Somehow she doubted it.

There was always another mission, another moment where evil could break through the thin membrane between this world and beyond. But the thought of sipping a crisp sauvignon blanc looking out to the blue horizon while the apocalypse went on without them was definitely tempting right now.

They turned off-road onto a track toward the beach, the Jeep jolting over rocks, bouncing up and down on the stones. Morgan winced as every bump scraped her shorts over the burns on her legs. She turned her face away to look out the window, hiding her expression as pain lanced through her.

Jake didn't know the extent of her injuries, and she had tried to keep it that way, but the salt water would be excruciating on her burns. She couldn't go down there, she couldn't dive. She couldn't be the partner he needed, but she didn't know how to tell him.

CHAPTER 18

AMADO PARKED THE JEEP a few meters from the waves lapping the shore and jumped out, gathering the gear together in the back.

Morgan and Jake got out and went around to help him.

"This will be a great dive," Amado said with his trademark enthusiasm. "I can guide you to the best places. Whatever you want to see."

Jake looked over at Morgan, and she caught his eye. It was forbidden to go inside the sunken church, but that's where they needed to look.

"I don't think you need to come down with me, Amado," Jake said. "Morgan and I will be fine on our own. We're experienced divers."

Morgan thought back to their dive in the Dead Sea in Israel as she looked out at the horizon of the turquoise sea. It seemed so long ago now, and she ached to get into the blue water.

"You gearing up?" Jake called over.

Morgan had to tell him, but she hated to put into words the weakness that held her back. Jake wanted her by his side because she was his partner, his equal as an ARKANE agent, and now she was going to let him go down alone on a dangerous dive on the edge of a volcanic island.

Jake walked toward her, his face quizzical, the corkscrew scar at his temple tightening as he looked at her with a question in his eyes. "What is it?"

Morgan took a deep breath. "My burns. You don't know how bad they are. I can't go in … the dressings …"

"The pain." Jake took her hand, his amber eyes filled with understanding. "The salt-water would be excruciating. I'm happy to go down alone, it's no problem. Or Amado can come with me." He paused. "You should have told me before."

Morgan sighed. "I hate to let you down."

"Remember when I lay in hospital, and you went off to Egypt without me on the quest for the Ark of the Covenant?"

Morgan nodded.

"Did you think any worse of me for not going with you?"

She shook her head. "Of course not. You were injured. But this isn't the same –"

"It *is* the same." Jake leaned closer to her. "If you came down with me, you could get us both into trouble. The stronger move is to stay up here and keep watch."

"Then I'll gladly take the stronger move."

But Morgan's heart sank as she watched Jake gear up, wishing that she was going down there too. Every breath he took underwater without her was time that she should be next to him.

Plus, she really fancied some tropical diving in the cool blue sea.

Jake walked over to Amado and pulled an envelope filled with US dollars from his pack. "I need you to come down as my buddy and take me to the church. But we need to be clear." He handed the envelope over. "I'm looking for something, and if I find it, you don't know about it. You never saw it."

Amado opened the envelope, his eyes widening at the cash inside. He nodded. "Of course, I'll take you wherever you want to go."

Morgan felt a twinge of guilt at the bribery, but they had no time to get the proper permits. Martin could sort out details with the Filipino government later if they found what they were looking for. Director Marietti had useful contacts at all levels of the Catholic Church. When ARKANE was on a mission, approval for tomb-raiding was not usually an issue. The problem was finding the right tomb.

While Jake and Amado readied the gear, Morgan stood at the water's edge, shoes off, sinking her toes into the sand as she relished the soft touch of the ocean. A huge cross marked the site of the sunken village offshore with a viewing platform around its edge for tourists to look down at the shallower ruins. The cross stood high out of the water pointing toward the heavens, resting on the remains of the city that lay beneath the waves. A memorial to the dead that drew people to the site even though it was inevitable that the volcano would erupt again one day. An island born of fire would never escape its fate to die in the same way.

No one knew when, but it would happen.

It put life in perspective, and Morgan considered how crazy it was that Naomi's life hung in the balance because of a set of tiny finger bones. The relics needed to be retrieved, but Naomi was just as precious to the ARKANE team as Martin or Jake was. So, they would find the relics and deliver them to the man who held her hostage. Dead bone was surely not worth a life.

Morgan turned back to help Amado and Jake load up an outrigger kayak with the dive gear. Amado threw in a spearfishing gun at the last moment.

He grinned. "There might be time to find dinner after the dive. A barbecue on the beach is a great way to finish the day."

They pushed the outrigger into the surf and Amado paddled them out to the cross. Morgan clambered out onto the platform while the young man tied the boat as they finished gearing up.

* * *

Jake sat on the side of the outrigger putting on his dive gear. He looked back at Morgan, her face forlorn as she looked down at them. She loved to scuba-dive, and to be honest, she had a lot more experience than he did. Her Israeli military training stretched to scuba reconnaissance whereas he had only dived on a few missions. The diving in South Africa was hardly gentle, with dangerous waters and great white sharks, so he hadn't logged too many hours underwater.

Perhaps one day when they got round to that glass of wine in a hot pool, he and Morgan might dive together somewhere peaceful.

He dangled his feet in the warm sea and looked down through the blue water at the ruins beneath. It was so clear that he could see fish swimming around watery silhouettes of crosses covered in coral. The graveyard turned artificial reef was just another place to hunt or hide, where life continued in its perpetual cycle.

Jake tested his regulator, taking a breath of bottled air, then checked the readings on his dive computer and partially inflated his BCD, buoyancy control device. He checked he had everything he needed in the catch bag. Everything looked good. He made the OK signal to Amado, first finger and thumb together in an 'O' shape. Then he turned and made the same signal to Morgan. She gave it back to him and smiled, waving goodbye.

Jake held his mask on his face and slipped forward into the water. He sank quickly, and a meter or so down he added a few puffs of air to his BCD, coming to neutral buoyancy so that he hovered above the seafloor. He looked up to the shimmering line of the surface above as it was broken by Amado coming down to meet him, his body perfectly aligned and comfortable in the sea.

The young man pointed to deeper waters, and they finned gently over the graveyard. Jake enjoyed the sensation of his body suspended in the blue, the feeling of flying as strong strokes of his fins propelled him over the crosses beneath. The memorials all pointed in different directions, undulating across the uneven seafloor disrupted by the volcanic eruption. The buried graveyard was eerie in the azure light of the water, dappled sun turning algae bright green as if covered in lush grass.

A shoal of tiny baitfish suddenly darted past in formation, flashing silver as they headed for the surface. Perhaps driven by something beneath.

Jake glanced around, wary for predators. Sharks were regularly seen in these waters, but he could only see two large Moorish Idols peeking out from behind one of the crosses, their elongated top fins fanning out behind them. Lion-fish prowled near the bottom of the seafloor, and inquisitive Rainbow Wrasse darted alongside the divers as they swam toward the buried church.

A garden of Banded Sea Kraits hung in the water, their slender bodies waving with the current as it washed over and around them. Amado guided Jake further away, so as not to disrupt their calm dance.

They passed over a giant clam, its fleshy lips of iridescent blue open to the water, its shell covered in pink mottled coral. The natural curves and wavy edges stood out against the straight lines of manmade stone nearby. Jake wished he had more time, that he could investigate the secrets of this underwater sanctuary, but he had the mission in mind.

Find the relics and get to Naomi.

Amado guided Jake away from the main section of the graveyard, descending to the old church. It had collapsed sideways in the water over time, much of it subsided into ruin. Amado pointed down and shook his head as if there were no chance to find a way in.

Jake dived down and examined the ruins, hovering in the water as he swam around. Part of an archway stood on its side leading into what remained of the nave. There was an opening that he could get through. It would be tight, but it was possible.

He pointed down, indicating with hand signals that the two of them could swim inside. Amado paused, indecision in his eyes, then shook his head, clearly unwilling to proceed.

Not enough dollars for that, I guess. Jake finned alone to the opening.

He pulled the flashlight from his belt and gently eased himself through the stone archway into the church beyond.

A cloud of fish darted out of the gloom toward him. He started back in surprise, kicking up a cloud of sand that obscured his vision immediately.

First rule of cave diving. Don't kick up the sand.

It had been years since he'd done his first cave dives and the words of his instructor came flooding back even as Jake mentally kicked himself. Even though this was not a cave as such, it was still an overhead environment where he couldn't get to the surface quickly or easily. He shouldn't even be in there without a buddy and Jake wished Morgan was there beside him.

For a moment he thought about getting out of the enclosed space, but then he clenched his fists, steeling himself for the search. There was no way he was going back up there empty-handed.

The flashlight beam caught the edge of an altar further in, just a few meters away. Jake finned carefully toward it over large boulders and the remains of tombstones etched into gigantic flagstones beneath. The Spanish names evoked a long-gone era when men of faith traveled an unexplored world in search of fame and glory. A time of adventure into the uncharted. Now the terrestrial world was mostly mapped, photographed, exploited for resources, but there was still mystery out there. Perhaps even more down here in the depths.

The church looked like it had been looted a long time ago, not unexpected since it was so close to land and easily dived upon by locals and tourists alike. Anything of value would have been taken, but there was a chance that the relic had not been considered valuable, or that it still remained hidden, waiting for the right time to be discovered.

Jake thought of the bone vault under New Orleans and the symbol of the breath they had found repeated there. He examined the walls for markings, feeling his way around methodically until he had completed a circuit.

There was nothing.

He looked again at the tombstones below and tilted his body to descend, equalizing his ears so that he could skim along the bottom. Weed and sea grass grew from indented names, and the oldest tombs were almost completely obscured. He began to pull himself over them, checking each stone for anything useful.

As he swept a handful of sand away from one, Jake caught his breath in surprise.

The symbol of the breath carved into the tomb of a child.

Jake remembered the image of the map Luis Rey had sent them. The bones that formed the countries were tiny, intricate. He wondered how many of the bones came from children of Empire, lives used and forgotten in the march for progress.

He brushed away the rest of the sand and felt around the edge of the tombstone, then reached for the catch bag attached to his belt and pulled out a chisel with a long handle.

Jake worked the sharp end under the edge of the tombstone. It slid under, and he levered it up to lift the stone away from the floor, then wedged the end of the chisel in. A small metal casket gleamed under his flashlight beam, etched with the whorls and eddies of the wind around a cross of bone.

The breath of God.

The casket could contain the remains of a long-dead

Spanish child, or it could contain a finger bone, part of the Hand of Ezekiel. There was only one way to find out.

Jake put one hand on the tombstone and began to ease it back –

A sudden explosion boomed through the water.

Seconds later, a shock wave propelled Jake back against the hard rock of the altar, his back arching over it, the force slamming the air from his lungs.

Huge blocks of stone dropped down from the roof above as the church began to collapse, driving silt up into the water, obscuring everything in the chamber.

Jake couldn't see anything. His mind whirled with questions, thoughts of Morgan and Amado outside. He fought to catch his breath as he dumped the air from his BCD.

He sank to the bottom, using blocks of stone to claw himself back to the tiny grave. He pulled out the casket and shoved it into his catch bag, clipping it to his belt.

He dragged himself toward the exit, using his flashlight to try and find the way he came in. But as he shone the beam up, a chill ran down his spine. Boulders dislodged by the explosion completely blocked the archway.

He was trapped.

CHAPTER 19

MINUTES BEFORE, MORGAN HEARD the revving of a motorboat approaching around the headland. She ducked down below the parapet and peeked around the side of the platform, using the outrigger to shield herself from view.

A white motorboat hurtled into the bay, two Filipino men at the helm. One pointed at the outrigger and then out to deeper waters in the direction that Jake and Amado had gone. Morgan couldn't understand the Tagalog language, but their tone was threatening. They were definitely not tourists.

The boat accelerated out toward the underwater church, and Morgan could only watch in horror as one of the men dropped a device into the water.

The other man revved the boat and sped off as fast as possible.

A moment later, a massive explosion rocked the seafloor.

A rumble came from below, then a huge plume of water erupted from the dive site. The whole platform rocked as giant waves battered the cross, washing over the deck.

Morgan stayed crouched down even as the water washed over her, fighting to keep her hold on the platform. She was soaked through, salt water seeping through her bandages, sharp pain pulsing as her muscles tensed ready for action. She thought of Jake down there, possibly injured, possibly

… But there was no time to think about that now.

The motorboat revved again, swinging in a wide arc, coming back to check the outrigger. Morgan reached down into the boat, quickly grabbing the speargun that Amado had stashed earlier. She slipped back behind the parapet, calming her breathing as she checked the mechanism of the weapon.

It was only good for one shot.

The sound of the motorboat grew closer, and the men pulled up next to the platform, talking rapidly. One climbed into the outrigger. They were clearly looking for something.

Morgan inched back behind the parapet. Perhaps they would leave without seeing her.

One of the men made a comment, the other sounded confused. Morgan almost groaned aloud as she realized that one BCD and tank remained in the boat. The men must know that one person hadn't gone down.

Suddenly, they went quiet.

Morgan slipped softly around the back of the cross, so the giant structure was between her and the intruders.

One man stayed in the boat while the other stepped onto the platform, his wet footsteps slapping against the stone. She couldn't see him, but Morgan could only assume that he had a weapon stretched out in front.

She had one chance.

She closed her eyes, listening to the footsteps as the man came closer. For a moment she was back in the ambush holes of the Golan Heights as part of the Israeli Defense Force. She was a warrior. She was trained for this.

Although to be fair, she had never used a speargun for this purpose before.

The man's footsteps rounded the side of the cross.

Morgan thrust up hard from the ground toward him. She smashed the butt end of the speargun under his chin, thrusting his head back. He stumbled, raised his weapon, and she hammered the end of the speargun down on his hand.

He dropped the weapon, and she kicked it back behind her into the water.

A gunshot pinged against the cross, the man in the boat shouting as he fired.

Morgan angled herself behind the structure, using the speargun to jab at her attacker's belly. As he doubled over, she swung the heavy end across his temple.

The man sagged to the deck as another gunshot whizzed past, just missing her.

Morgan hunkered down and crawled around the side of the cross, staying low, staying out of sight until the last moment.

She stood and shot the speargun at the man in the boat, cable trailing behind it.

He looked down in surprise, clutching at the metal shaft embedded in his belly. He crumpled, toppling over the side of the boat into the water face down, a pool of blood spreading out around him.

Morgan gazed out toward the dive site. Jake and Amado hadn't surfaced. They must be in trouble. She would have to go down there, regardless of the pain. She should have gone in the first place. She clambered into the outrigger and started to check the remaining dive gear.

Movement caught her eye in the water a few meters away.

The dark silhouette of a tiger shark swimming toward the bloody corpse of the man she had just killed.

* * *

Down below, Jake swam up close to the rocks blocking the entrance, testing each with a firm hand as he tried to work out what had happened. Someone must have dropped an explosive device. Amado had been out in the open water. He would have been blown away from the scene by the blast, perhaps concussed, perhaps worse. And Morgan ... Jake had to get back up there.

He tried all the stones, but they were stuck fast, an immovable wall. There was no exit this way.

He looked down at his dive computer, checked his air supply. He had used a lot in his search, and there wasn't much remaining. He had to get out of here.

Jake calmed his breath, conserving air by breathing slowly, then thought about the design of the church that Martin had sent, plans from when the Spanish had been here. Turning in the water, he tried to orientate himself to where the various parts of the church had been. Part of the nave was buried, but there was a chance that one of the antechambers might still have an exit.

He finned to the west of the church, feeling around the walls, his fingers skimming over rough stone. Silt made the chamber as dark as the grave, and his flashlight had dimmed with so much use. Jake tried not to think about what would happen if the light went out, if he ended up trapped in here, buried like the thousands who died in the eruption.

There was no way for Morgan to get him out in time.

But then he looked down at the flashlight. It was still just about daylight topside. If he made it completely dark in here, perhaps he might see a crack of light from outside, a way to escape.

Jake turned the flashlight off and hung in the water, trying to relax in neutral buoyancy so as not to disturb the silt anymore. He closed his eyes, getting used to the darkness. As his breath came in, he rose a little in the water column. As he exhaled, he sank down. He imagined the air bladders of his lungs filling and emptying in a calm meditation.

After a few breaths, he opened his eyes. Everything was still dark. There was no way out.

Then from the corner of the church, he glimpsed a tiny chink of light.

Jake finned over and found that the explosion had blocked one entrance but also blown out another. It was still covered by a few large rocks, but he could make the hole bigger.

It was hard work, his breath ragged as he shifted the debris, effort straining his muscles.

Suddenly, he tried to take a breath and sucked on nothing. He grabbed his dive computer. No more air in the tank.

Jake pulled the final few stones away and tried to swim through the gap. His tank caught. He was stuck fast. He twisted and writhed, but he couldn't get through. His lungs began to ache.

With his breath almost out, Jake shrugged off his BCD leaving the tank behind. He wriggled out through the gap in the wall, pulling the catch bag out with him as he swam for the surface. As he rose, he let the remaining air trickle from his mouth in tiny bubbles as his lungs expanded.

A huge shadow passed overhead.

Jake looked up to see a tiger shark swimming above, heading for a bloody body in the water. He couldn't go directly to the surface, but he was desperate for breath.

The tiger shark worried at the corpse, biting chunks from it, leaving a trail of gore in the water. There would be more sharks coming.

Jake could see the silhouette of the outrigger a little further away and swam for it, holding his breath for as long as possible, trying not to swim in a panicked manner like a dying fish but slow and steady so as not to attract the shark. Finally, he surfaced next to the platform, gasping for breath.

Morgan pulled him from the water. "Thank goodness you made it. I was so worried."

Jake lay panting on the platform, gulping at the air, his chest heaving. Once he could breathe properly again, he noticed the body of a man behind the cross. "Looks like you managed alright up here."

Morgan sat back on her heels. "Amado?"

Jake shook his head. "I didn't see him. I was trapped in the church when the explosion happened. I had to leave another way."

The sun was beginning to set, the sky turning shades of tropical pink and orange. Feeding time for sharks, the apex predators of the reef.

Morgan stood up and looked toward the dive site. "The blast might have pushed him further out." She climbed into the outrigger. "I'll see if I can find him. We can't leave his body for the sharks."

* * *

She paddled away from the cross, looking down into the water at the silhouettes beneath. Most were reef sharks, not really dangerous, but a pack of them could tear a body to pieces soon enough.

Morgan paddled further out over the sunken cemetery until she saw the edge of the drop-off where the ruined church lay, then searched in circles spreading away from the site, looking down into the water then out to the horizon.

Just as she was about to turn back, Morgan saw a dark shadow hanging in the water a few meters away. Amado was face up, held upright by his BCD, but his head was slumped sideways, eyes closed.

The fin of a shark broke the water nearby.

Morgan slammed her paddle down, making as much noise as she could. The shark angled away, but she knew it would circle and return. She didn't have much time.

She paddled over quickly to the guide and bent over the side of the outrigger. Morgan grabbed Amado's BCD straps and heaved him onboard. His outstretched arms fell across the burns on her thighs and she bit back a scream of pain as he slid off, rasping the dressings over her weeping wounds.

Pushing aside the pain, Morgan paddled quickly back to the cross. Jake helped pull Amado's body out onto the platform and started CPR on the young man.

A few breaths and Amado coughed, vomiting seawater as he rolled over on one side, retching it all up.

Morgan sat next to him. "It's OK, you're alright. Just rest now."

When he had finally stopped coughing, Amado sat with his back against the cross. His eyes slowly focused on them and the man lying prone nearby.

"What happened?"

Morgan pointed at the motorboat. "Two men came in that and dropped an explosive device on the dive site. You're lucky to have made it back. Didn't end so well for them."

Jake went round to the body and turned the man over, so he lay face down revealing a tattoo on the back of his neck. A cross with the wind blowing around it. "These men were Brotherhood of the Breath." Jake looked up at Morgan, hope in his eyes.

"This must be the right place," she said.

"I found something down there." Jake scooted back round to his catch bag, opened it up and pulled out the casket from the church.

Morgan examined the patina of age on the surface. "We should probably wait until we're in a protected environment to open it."

Jake shook his head. "We need to know now. If the relic's not in here, then we have to keep looking."

He grabbed a dive knife and edged up the side of the box. It was filled with a dark red chunky liquid. They all leaned back, coughing as the noxious stench of decay wafted out. Jake slammed the lid back down.

"Guess that answers the question. It's Spanish cadaver soup."

Morgan leaned forward again. "You can't be sure. We need to pour out that liquid, check underneath."

Amado grimaced. "Seriously. That's gross."

Jake put the box on the edge of the platform and tipped it, with the lid held against the side, so the foul-smelling liquid dripped down into the sea. The sharks beneath went into a frenzy at the smell of death in the water.

As he poured, Jake felt something hard clunk against the lid. He turned the casket back up and took the lid off again. An object lay inside coated in fetid slime.

A finger bone, stoppered with red wax.

Morgan looked up at Jake, her eyes wide. "It must've been buried with a corpse all those years ago. But the water got inside."

She put on a dive glove and picked out the finger bone, sloshing fresh water over it, examining the seal. It didn't look like it had leaked.

"That's what you wanted?" Amado said, confusion in his voice. "I thought you were hunting for gold or treasure."

Jake looked over at him. "It's valuable to us."

Amado smiled. "Well, now you've found it, I can take you to the hot pools. You can have that glass of wine. I certainly need a drink."

Jake hesitated, and for a moment Morgan thought he was going to agree. But he shook his head. "Sorry, the party's over. We need to get back to the airport. We have a long way to travel tonight."

CHAPTER 20

Lima, Peru.

MORGAN LOOKED UP AT the Spanish baroque towers of the San Francisco Basilica as the warm sun of the morning blessed her skin. The air was cooler here, sweeping onto the Peruvian coastal plain from the Pacific and she felt dislocated, as if her soul were still back in the Philippines while her body was here, thousands of miles away.

Martin had managed to get them on a military transfer, not the comfiest of rides but certainly the fastest. She had snatched some sleep, aided by a handful of painkillers, fresh bandages and industrial earplugs. The roar of the engines still filled her ears, now overtaken by the capital city waking up. Cars on the highway, the chink of coffee cups and scrape of chairs from nearby cafés, the shouts of street vendors. She could understand them, the Spanish slightly different to her father's native country, but still similar enough.

Like the language, the church in front of her seemed strangely familiar. It was a slice of Europe in a far-flung land, testament to the extraordinary empire that brought death to so many as well as a new way of life that still shaped the culture hundreds of years later. Lima had been founded by the Spanish conquistador, Pizarro, in the sixteenth century, an important city that was home to the oldest functioning university in the Americas and still remained an important trading hub.

"The cathedral is dedicated to Saint Jude," Jake said as he walked up, handing Morgan a cup of steaming black coffee.

She smiled. "Patron saint of lost causes. Seems appropriate."

Morgan took a sip, allowing the bitter black to restore her energy drop by drop. She could travel the world, fight demons and evil men alike, but she couldn't go long without her coffee. She looked up at the two bell towers of yellow stucco over stone flanking an ornate sculptured door into the compound. Pigeons roosted in the cracks between the levels, their soft cooing a welcome for weary travelers.

"This place has an ossuary and a world-renowned library. If we're going to find any trace of the relic, it has to be here." She looked at her watch. "Martin's librarian contact, Father Alejandro, should be ready for us now."

They walked around the back of the main entrance to a tiny door designed for those who worked in the complex and delivered to the building. Father Alejandro stood watching two little wrens darting in and out of the branches of a Cinchona tree on the edge of the Parque de la Muralla, their sweet song filling the air. He wore the habit of the Franciscans, a simple brown robe with a humble *cincture* of rope belted around his slim waist. It had the customary three knots representing the vows of poverty, chastity and obedience, but with one difference. A bunch of keys hung down, some elaborately fashioned and others more modern in style.

He turned at their approach and stretched out his hands, a smile on his weathered face. "Welcome, you must be the friends of Martin."

His gesture of friendship made Morgan's heart glad.

Despite what she and Jake had experienced at the hands of people of extremist faith, most believers welcomed the stranger. They all shook hands.

"Martin told me that you seek the records of any friar who came from Spain back in the days of Empire. I have taken the liberty of getting those records for you. They wait in the reading room. This way."

Father Alejandro led them through the corridors of the monastery, hung with paintings of dour monks and scenes from the old country in between decorative tiling and carved wooden panels. It was a long way from the humble beginnings of the Franciscan monasteries of Europe, and every inch recalled the lost grandeur of the Spanish Empire. They emerged into a brightly colored passageway with deep ochre walls, planted on either side with bright geraniums, and walked onward to finally reach a giant wooden door, carved with images of books intertwined with leaves and flowers.

Father Alejandro pushed open the door and gestured for them to enter. "Welcome to our library. I try not to commit the sin of pride, but every day I thank the Lord for allowing me to work here."

A luxurious array of books stacked in several levels on wooden shelves reached from the richly carpeted floor to the ornate coffered ceiling above. Spiral staircases led to the upper levels while intricate glass chandeliers cast a golden light over two straight-back chairs waiting for curious readers in the center. The library smelled of musty old pages with a faint undertone of furniture polish.

Morgan felt like she was back in Oxford studying in the Radcliffe Camera, a wealth of knowledge just waiting for her to open the pages and read. While she had wanted to stay in the Philippines to relax and recover, she now wanted to sink into this place for the love of research, delving into obscure parts of history and human knowledge, indulging in the addiction of learning.

"It's beautiful," she whispered. Her eyes darted around the room, lighting on cracked leather spines, reciting the words in her mind like an incantation. Perhaps here she was the true devotee, the real believer, whereas in front of religious icons, she felt nothing. Her father had sought God amongst the Hebrew letters of the Kabbalah. Perhaps she also found the divine in learning and knowledge.

Father Alejandro led them to the second level, up a spiral staircase with wooden beams that creaked as they walked.

"I know your friend Martin would love to get this collection digitalized, but that is a way off as yet. We have some rare books, religious chronicles from the priests who came here, as well as unique *incunabula* brought over by the Spanish."

Jake turned to Morgan, whispering his question. "What's *incunabula*?"

"Books or pamphlets printed in Europe before 1501." She stopped by one of the shelves, her fingers trailing across the gold etching of a Bible in Spanish.

Father Alejandro turned and caught her, his previously kind eyes suddenly flashing with possessive anger. Morgan jerked her hand away sharply as he composed himself, once again the genial monk. Jake examined another shelf of books and missed the glance, but Morgan found herself alert now, wondering whether the monk really welcomed them into his sanctuary.

"This way." Father Alejandro led them to a small room at the back of the library with wooden paneled walls. Four piles of record books lay on the table, each with sewn spines and leather covers, each as thick as the medieval table they lay upon. Two pairs of white gloves lay next to them.

Father Alejandro pointed at the books. "I know you don't have much time, but I trust you will find what you're looking for in these." He nodded to them. "I'll be down in the main hall. Please call if you need anything."

He turned and walked out, leaving Morgan and Jake looking down at the daunting pile of records. They put on the gloves, gearing up for the search.

Jake opened the first one, then the next. "They're in Spanish."

Morgan laughed. "What did you expect?"

"Maybe a computer with excellent search capability."

"If that had been available, Martin could have done this remotely, but this place doesn't welcome digitalization. Makes you wonder what's in here." Morgan sat down at the table and pulled the first tome toward her. "Spanish for finger is *dedo*, and bone is *hueso*. That should get you started. Or just look for anything around the right date."

They began to page through the record books, the finger pads of their white gloves soon dusty and discolored.

The minutes ticked away. The sun slowly moved across the windowpane until the shadows lengthened.

Jake opened one book and pointed out a map of the catacombs that lay beneath the cathedral. "How cool is this." He traced the corridors with a careful finger. "Just think of the monks carrying bodies back and forth down there for centuries."

Morgan sneezed, turning away as she did so. Then she pushed her chair back and stood up, stretching her back. "This is ridiculous. We don't even know if the right records are in here."

Jake held a hand up. "Wait a moment. This inventory records several hundred finger bones kept in the catacombs. Any of them could be the one we're looking for."

"Or none of them." Morgan went over to join him and looked down at the list. "Looks like relics from minor saints are all kept together in one shrine. Maybe it would be easier to go have a look?"

She walked back into the main library and found Father Alejandro bent close to a manuscript, examining an illuminated figure under a magnifying glass.

"Father?"

He jumped at her approach, startled from his reverie. Then his smile widened, as welcoming as ever. "What can I do for you?"

"The relic we're looking for might be part of the collection of finger bones held in the ossuary. Can we see them, please?"

A moment of hesitation and then Father Alejandro nodded. "I can take you down there. Although, of course, you can't touch the relics themselves, only pray at the shrine."

Jake walked out of the study room and together they descended into the main library. Father Alejandro led them to the back where a heavy door opened into a stone corridor beyond. It was almost dark outside now, and the small windows above let in little light, but the monk didn't falter, his footsteps sure in the shadows.

"The monastery is closed to tourists now, so we must be quiet as the monks ready themselves for evening prayer. I'll take you to the relics and then go join my brothers. Quickly now."

The monk scurried ahead, pulling the set of keys from his belt as they reached a heavy iron-bound door. He unlocked it and swung it open revealing a stone staircase winding down into darkness. A line of skulls stared back at them, empty eye sockets filled with the dust of the dead.

Morgan remembered waking in the catacombs of Paris surrounded by thousands of plague skeletons. She shivered a little at the thought of entering the winding corridors of bone below, but with Father Alejandro guiding the way, they would be out of here soon enough.

The monk reached behind the thick door and clicked on the light switch. They descended into the cool of the catacombs.

"The burial crypts were used for the dead as the city grew during colonial times," Father Alejandro explained as they walked. "They had mass burial pits for the common folk, but the nobles were buried separately until the early 1800s. Over 25,000 bodies were buried down here, their bones arranged in decorative ways. Curious to many in New Spain, but commonly used in Europe." He pointed into one chamber. "Have a look."

Morgan and Jake ducked inside and looked down at a circular pit ringed with long femur bones and skulls in concentric circles, spiraling toward a central mound of the dead.

"No finger bones," Jake whispered, his voice echoing through the halls.

"There are chambers filled with individual bones further along," Father Alejandro replied, his footsteps clicking on the stone as he moved on. "The relic shrines are beyond that."

Morgan and Jake ducked out, hurrying after the monk as he moved swiftly down the corridor, turning this way and that as the catacombs forked into new passageways. Morgan lost her bearings after the eighth or ninth turn, and soon they were in narrow tunnels far beyond the well-lit tourist route.

Father Alejandro finally stopped at a thick wooden door with a barred window. "These cells were used by early monks for their time of solitude, and now we keep some of the less popular relics here. No one comes down here anymore. You are the first in many years." He gestured into the cell. "Perhaps you will find what you seek inside."

Morgan entered the cell first and sure enough, arrayed in front of them were finger bones of all sizes, some wrapped in silk, some in reliquaries, others in crumbling piles.

Jake came in behind her, and the cell felt tiny with both of them in it. "Let's hope it's in here somewhere."

A metallic scrape on stone.

Morgan spun around as the monk slammed the cell door shut, locking them both inside.

CHAPTER 21

"What are you doing?" Morgan pushed past Jake, hands on the metal bars, shaking at the door.

Father Alejandro looked at her, his eyes blazing with anger, all sense of friendliness gone now. "You have brought this on yourselves. You'll rot down here with the relic you seek."

As he walked away, his robe shifted, and Morgan caught sight of a cross tattoo with the whirling wind on the back of his neck.

She tugged at the bars, shouting after the monk, her voice echoing down the stone corridor as he turned out of sight. "You can't leave us. Martin, our archivist, knows we're here. He'll send someone."

The monk's voice floated back to them. "You left hours ago, I helped as much as I could. You insisted on leaving, last seen headed to the most dangerous area of the city. By the time anyone finds you, your bones will be part of the relic shrine …"

His voice faded away.

Then the lights went out.

Jake clicked his flashlight on. "We should have known the Brotherhood was here. That guy was way too friendly." He bent to the pile of bones. "But he did say we'd rot down here with the relic we seek, so it might be in here somewhere."

He began to sift through the pile, examining each bone within its case, intent on checking the ends for a wax seal, seemingly oblivious to being locked inside.

Morgan looked around the cell. It was only a few meters square with walls of thick stone blocks. One door of thick wood with an ancient lock. No windows, unsurprising given how deep below the earth they were.

She bent to the mortar between two of the wall blocks. Perhaps they could chip it away, get into the next room, escape that way. She picked up a small bronze reliquary, dusty with age but with a sharp edge and used it to scrape at the grey mortar. A little bit flaked off but the walls were well built, and it would take forever.

Morgan sighed and went back over to the door, squeezing past Jake as he hunkered down. She examined the hinges. They were firmly embedded in the stone wall, impossible to break through. She slammed the heel of her hand against the lock mechanism, rattling it, but it stayed firm.

Jake's flashlight suddenly flickered, like a candle blown by an unseen wind.

Morgan spun around, panic rising within her at the thought of being down here in the dark. She imagined those finger bones coming to life, scratching away at their boxes, scraping away their silken wrappings, curling across the floor like skeletal worms. It made her flesh crawl.

She knelt by Jake as he shook the flashlight. "Do you have any other batteries?"

"No, but don't worry, we're going to make it out of here. Help me look through the rest of the pile. We'll find the relic, then we'll make a break for it."

Morgan shook her head in disbelief at his calm demeanor, but she sat down cross-legged and began to search through the pile of bones, recognizing that this self-doubt was unusual for her. The pain of her burns was a dull ache that sapped her strength, both physical and emotional. She was tired and more broken than she liked to admit and she hadn't allowed for it on the mission. Down here, she felt like more of a liability than a help to Jake. Perhaps he'd be better off with a new partner after all.

The flashlight flickered again, and they both froze.

It buzzed a little, then flared into brightness once more.

They moved more quickly now, examining each relic box and discarding them just as fast until suddenly, near the bottom of the pile, Jake pulled out a metal casket similar to the one from the Philippines. The lid was loose.

He pulled it off, but only the tatters of a red pillow lay inside as if a rat had made it home.

"There are loose bones at the bottom of the pile. Maybe it fell out." Morgan raked through the heap, a grimace on her face as she pulled apart the tangle of remains mixed in with rotted material and dead rodents. A glimmer of red caught her eye. A fat finger bone with scarlet wax on the end.

Morgan picked it out of the pile triumphantly, but then her heart sank. The wax was only a smear on one side. The hollow finger bone was empty, its precious contents long gone.

"All this way for nothing," Morgan sighed. "Worse than nothing now we're trapped here."

Jake shook his head. "It's not for nothing, we'll take it anyway. It matches the others, so we can still use it for trade." He picked up the relic and placed it in his pack along with the others. "And we're not trapped."

He picked up an ulna, a long arm bone, and smashed it against the wall. It shattered into long splinters on the floor. Jake chose a couple of the shards, thin picks with sharp ends. Walking over to the door, he maneuvered them into the lock mechanism and jimmied them up and down, listening for the click of tumblers in the ancient lock.

Morgan held the flickering flashlight as it began to fade again. "You sure you know what you're doing?"

He grinned. "Martin and I practiced this together after he got stuck in the vault that time. One of my many talents."

The lock clunked. Jake held the bones in place while Morgan heaved the door open.

They stepped out into the corridor just as the flashlight flared its last and went out.

Jake reached for Morgan's hand, and they clung to each other in the dark. A skittering sound came from the corridor ahead, the pitter patter of rats. Morgan wondered what they were gnawing on down here, grateful that it wouldn't be their bones.

If they could find their way out, of course.

"Do you know –" she whispered.

"Sshh, I'm concentrating. I'm trying to recall the map from earlier."

Morgan remembered the plan of the catacombs that Jake had discovered in the record book. He had traced the lines of the underground tunnels with a finger but could he recall enough to guide them out of here in the dark?

Jake took a tentative step forward, her hand tight in his. Whatever happened, they would be together.

He started walking more confidently, Morgan behind him, one hand on the wall, the other on his belt. When they reached a corner, he turned left with no hesitation, their footsteps echoing through the catacombs as they walked on.

Eventually, a warm glow of light came from up ahead, and they hurried toward it. In a chapel dedicated to the dead, an image of the crucified Savior looked down upon them, lit by an electric lamp representing the eternal flame.

Morgan exhaled, letting out the breath she hadn't even realized she'd been holding. Relief flooded over her and exhaustion began to rise. She leaned against the wall, resting her head against the stone.

"We're almost there," Jake said. "This chamber is below the nave of the church. Do you need to rest a moment?"

She shook her head. "I'm OK, and I don't think we should hang around. Father Alejandro might not be the only member of the Brotherhood here. Besides, it's night already, and we have to be in San Francisco tomorrow." She looked up at him. "Unless you want to go on alone. I know I'm slowing you down."

Jake smiled, the lamplight giving his eyes a tawny glow. "We're partners. We go together."

He reached for her hand, and they walked out of the catacombs up into the church above and into the night.

* * *

San Francisco, USA.

Jake stood on the pier at the back of the Ferry Building looking out toward the Oakland Bay Bridge, its metal spars rising out of the brilliant blue water. Squat ferryboats chugged back and forth, disgorging passengers into the downtown city area. Raucous seagulls hopped across the ground, pecking at leftovers from the lunchtime rush that eased as the afternoon wore on. The air smelled of salt and vinegar from discarded chips overlaid with fresh sourdough bread from a nearby bakery.

Morgan lay on a bench in a patch of sun near the water's edge, her eyes closed, a moment of peace in their crazy adventure. She had the military ability of catching zees wherever she was, sleeping easily then waking in an instant, alert for danger. Jake looked down at her, wanting to brush the dark curls from her brow but knowing that if he moved closer, she would sense him there. He satisfied himself by watching over her, giving her a little time to recover. Her angular face was pinched, and she'd lost weight that she couldn't afford to. It was clear that she carried constant pain in her body and Jake knew how that felt. He wished he could take some of it from her.

He rechecked his phone. The text message had arrived just as they'd landed.

Midnight. Alcatraz. Bring the five relics.

The problem was that they only had four – Toledo, New Orleans, the Philippines, Lima. They needed the last finger to complete the Hand of Ezekiel, and even then, Jake wasn't sure how it was supposed to work when one was broken and empty.

Of course, they could go to Alcatraz all guns blazing, take Naomi back and forget the bones. But the mission, as always, went beyond saving individual lives. ARKANE's primary purpose was the recovery and protection of relics, books of ancient knowledge and objects of power that would outlive generations. A human life was but a drop in the river of life, a spark quickly fading in the night, whereas these artifacts could change the course of the river itself.

Director Marietti had made it clear that their first priority was the Hand of Ezekiel. It must rest in the ARKANE vault within the box of bone that Luis Rey held. So they needed to finish the search and go to the rendezvous point, but with a different agenda than expected.

Jake looked down at Morgan. He hadn't told her of Marietti's hard line – she had enough problems with the Director's seeming disregard for human life – but he hoped she would be ready. He needed her on Alcatraz tonight.

But first, they needed that final finger bone.

He pulled out a map of San Francisco, the rustle of paper waking Morgan. She sat up and stretched like a cat, arching her back and rolling her shoulders. Jake caught the tightening in her jaw as she stood, the bandages on her legs shifting as she moved. He turned back to the map, giving her space, understanding that she didn't want a witness to her pain.

"I'm still trying to decide where we should look first."

He pointed at a green expanse flanking the entrance to the Golden Gate Bridge. "This is the Presidio, a fortified base that the Spanish established and a military area until recently. It's now a national park, but it still has a cemetery." He moved his finger down the page to a tiny sliver of green in the Mission District. "This is Mission Dolores, established by Junípero Serra as one of a chain of missions up the West Coast."

Morgan leaned over the map, her dark curls brushing against Jake's neck, her breath on his skin. He could smell the coconut scent of her shampoo, and he wanted to lean back against her.

"It's got to be the Mission first. Maybe the relic is just sitting there, waiting for us." She shrugged. "You never know. Sometimes it really is that simple."

* * *

They jumped in an Uber, the easiest way to get around the city, and headed inland past high-rises and smart hotels across the city blocks. Morgan noticed how many homeless people begged on the street, the uncomfortable juxtaposition of some of the wealthiest people in America next to the rejected and outcast.

The streets changed as they drove into the Mission District, the sound of Latino music drifting out of eclectic stores, tattoo parlors and independent shops with handmade gifts next to unusual flavors of ice cream. Morgan found it dislocating to be in the USA, a culture at once so close to Europe and yet sometimes so jarringly different. Yet in this part of the city, she felt a sense of belonging, as if the Spanish heritage called to the part of her that shared a common ancestor.

The Uber pulled up on a corner next to an elaborate basilica, its twin bell towers and facade a faded cream that looked almost golden in the afternoon sun. Elaborate designs covered a vaulted entranceway with columns twisting toward heaven, drawing the eye up to the canopy of blue sky above.

Morgan looked up in confusion. "This can't be the place. It's too modern."

Then she noticed the humble white adobe chapel next door that most would walk past without a second glance. In Spain, she had grown used to massive cathedrals, testament to the riches of the all-powerful Church, but this basic mission house looked exactly as it must have done back in 1776.

Jake walked over to the historical plaque on the wall. "It's the oldest building in San Francisco, established as part of the California chain of missions, dedicated to Saint Francis of Assisi. Apparently, they even bless animals here at a special service once a year. Very cool."

An open door led into a tourist shop where a plump woman sat watching a Latino soap opera. She glanced up as they entered and took their entrance fee quickly, waving them through into the Mission.

The modest chapel was empty, its few wooden pews laid out before an altar at the front of the church, flanked by statues of Franciscan friars. Chevrons of terracotta red and mustard yellow marked the wooden panels above the sanctuary, muted colors of the earth that added intensity to the gold statues beneath.

It smelled faintly of incense left behind after a service, but it was clear that the grand basilica further on was the main center of worship now, and this basic chapel had been left behind along with the vows of those who established it. After all, poverty didn't fit so well with the American dream.

Morgan looked up at the vaulted roof above her head, the dark wooden beams lashed together with rawhide. She could almost hear the hammer blows and the rasping sound of the saw as converts built the church in this new corner of

Empire. Their work had changed the course of history, but some claimed that Junípero Serra was behind the mistreatment of local Native American peoples, who saw hard labor, the spread of disease and forced conversions as oppression. The workers had lived in appalling conditions, women raped and beaten, families packed into tight living quarters as they were forced to serve the newly arrived Spanish. One historian had even called the missions, "a series of picturesque charnel houses," and Junípero Serra was responsible for them.

Such a man could not possibly be a saint, and yet, in 2015, Pope Francis had canonized the friar. Despite the protests against his sainthood, Junípero Serra now interceded with God on behalf of those still on earth.

But it looked like part of him remained.

A reliquary stood next to the altar, an ornate golden cross with a thick central pillar containing space for a relic at its heart. An ivory pillow decorated with scarlet thread lay in the middle surrounding a glass case with a bone of the saint inside.

Morgan called across to Jake as she pointed it out. "Told you. Sometimes it's just that easy."

They walked closer to the relic, Morgan's smile fading as she saw what lay within.

CHAPTER 22

MORGAN BENT CLOSER TO the glass. What had looked like a finger was just another vial containing a sliver of bone, such a tiny relic for a place that loomed large over the religious history of the city.

She sighed as she straightened up, looking around the church for any other shrine. There was nothing. "I guess an easy ride was too much to hope for."

They walked around to the museum behind the chapel on the edge of a peaceful rose garden leading to the cemetery beyond. Old pictures of the Mission over the years sat next to a Franciscan habit, original construction tools, and even a doll from one of the children who had been raised here.

Morgan thought back to the statue of Junípero Serra in Palma, Majorca, where the priest stood with his hand on the head of a Native American boy wearing a loin-cloth. The interpretation of history was on a knife-edge here and as ever, both sides owned a part of the truth. Some children would have benefitted from the Mission, their lives changed for the better. Others would have found it a living hell. The same dichotomy applied to her own home country of Israel, and no single person's experience could capture the complications of a nation's past.

Jake stood by the door, ignoring the history around him

while he scanned the research material Martin had sent over on his phone.

"This is odd," he said. "Although Junípero Serra's body is buried at the Carmel Mission, it seems that over five hundred relics were offered to believers before he was canonized."

Morgan frowned. "What do you mean?" She went over to look at the pictures.

Expecting more historical black and white images, Morgan was surprised to see a middle-aged woman with efficient short hair and a Bible in hand standing in front of a glass case. She wore jeans and an oversized baggy shirt that hugged her significant figure, and she pointed at the relic with a smile that implied ownership.

"This woman is a theology teacher," Jake read. "Just one of hundreds of believers who own a Serra relic. They were apparently offered in exchange for donations back in the 1990s – not for sale, of course."

"Of course." Morgan raised an eyebrow. "Any clue as to who might have got a finger bone?"

Jake scrolled through the page. "Martin hacked into the Catholic accounts for the area and listed the amount donated for each of the relics. I guess the more money, the more impressive the relic?"

"Makes sense." Morgan pointed at the screen. "What's that one?"

An eye-watering sum had been donated by the Woodberry family with a description that was slightly different than most. It listed 'bone' instead of 'fragment.'

Jake zoomed in to read more. "San Francisco stopped burials within the city limits in 1900, moving many dead out to Colma, south of the city. But the Woodberrys kept a vault for the family bones not so far away."

They headed out into the sun again and called another Uber. It drew up in front of the mission house within a minute, testament to the sheer number of drivers in the city, and they drove back to the north side skirting the edge of Golden Gate Park.

As they idled at a stop light, Morgan looked out the window to see a family cycle past, a toddler in a seat behind her dad, her little face staring back at the strange lady in the taxi.

Morgan smiled and waved, thinking of her niece Gemma back at home on the outskirts of Oxford. They sometimes went for a ride in the Botanical Gardens, the little girl thrilled to smell the flowers and run after pigeons with squeals of delight. Morgan would do anything for Gemma, but would she try to conquer death itself?

She had raged against Father Ben's death, but she would never consider trying to bring him back. The body was merely a shell, after all, and she had seen enough dead bodies to know that the life inside wasn't contained by flesh after it had failed them. Her father had believed that a spark of the divine lived within each person and returned to the source at death, but then as a Kabbalist Jew, he also believed in the resurrection of the physical body.

Death was complicated, but it was also certain, and those who fought against that certainty must surely find themselves "raging against the dying of the light," as the poet Dylan Thomas wrote. The constant pain of her burns on this mission gave Morgan a taste of mortality, a sense that one day her body would fail her, and she would not rise to fight another day. But for now, she would continue on by Jake's side.

The Uber drove on, pulling into what looked like a residential street, but the houses with their proud American flags masked the true nature of the area. At the end of the road, a ceremonial archway with a metal-barred gate led into the grounds of the San Francisco Columbarium.

"You want me to wait?" the driver said, looking dubiously at the sign for the funeral home.

"No, we're good," Jake said as they left the taxi and walked into the parking lot, looking up at the Columbarium. It was a circular, Neo-classical building with a copper-domed roof surrounded by red and white sculpted rose bushes that reminded Morgan of Alice in Wonderland. *Off with their heads*, she thought, wondering about the human remains inside.

An old African-American man inched around the building, sweeping every section with great care, his gnarled hands holding the stiff brush like it was a precious object. He wore a tool-belt with pruning shears poking out, clearly responsible for the meticulous upkeep of the place.

He looked up at their approach. "Welcome friends. I'm Horace, the caretaker. Any questions, you just ask."

Morgan smiled. "We're looking for a family tomb."

Horace's face lit up. "Well, I've been here thirty years so I know all of them. Who you looking for?"

"The Woodberrys. We've come all the way from England to see their last resting place."

Horace nodded. "I know them." He waved them over. "This way."

They walked along a concrete path flanked by green grass with perfectly trimmed edges. It was a far cry from the higgledy-piggledy graveyards of Britain and felt somehow like a Disney equivalent, as if death should be fastidiously tidy, and grief corralled into something tame.

There were plaques on the walls behind the bushes. One read *Dorothea Klumpke Roberts, Astronomer. She loved the stars too fondly to be fearful of the night.* Morgan wondered if Dorothea's ashes were responsible for the beautiful colors and scent of the roses. She hoped so.

Horace led them to the main door and propped up his broom next to it. "This was once part of the Odd Fellows Cemetery with over 167 acres for burials and later a crematorium, but after the city prohibited burials and then cremation, they established the cemetery in Colma."

Jake started in recognition. "Didn't the Odd Fellows have a cemetery in New Orleans as well?"

Horace nodded, his enthusiasm evident for historical places. "Oh yes, it's mostly closed to the public now, but you can still get in there if you know the password." He tapped the side of his nose and laughed, a deep belly sound that made Morgan smile with his contagious joy. This man had clearly made peace with death, and that gave her hope.

He pushed the door open, and they went inside. The entrance hall was low and dark, but then the circular space opened out into a spacious central hall with three gallery levels filled with glass-fronted niches, each with an urn or casket inside holding the remains of a life. Decorative columns stretched up to a pink and blue ornate dome with an oculus window through which the late sunlight filtered down, casting shadows across the marble floor. Stained glass windows around the sides let in more light and the place smelled of fresh flowers and furniture polish.

Horace pulled a chamois cloth from his belt to wipe a speck of dust from one of the glass panels. Morgan hoped that when he passed, someone would tend to his grave as carefully as he did for others.

"There are 8500 niches in here," Horace explained. "There's still some space if you're interested." He laughed again. "Your Woodberrys are up in Argo on the second level. You can go that way." He pointed to a small staircase. "I'll leave you awhile. Just holler if you need anything."

He walked back out again, adjusting a vase of flowers on the way, so they were perfectly symmetrical.

Morgan turned to take in the expanse of the levels, noting the classical symbolism that dominated the design. Rooms on the ground floor were named after the winds: Zephyrus, Olympias, Auster. On the upper levels, Sothis, an Egyptian goddess associated with Sirius, the brightest star in the sky, sat next to Argo, the mythological ship that Jason used to find the Golden Fleece. It was a classical history in architecture, such a surprising place to discover in the heart of what had become almost a futurist city.

Shadows faded and the chamber darkened. Clouds thickened above the oculus as the bright day faded into the beginnings of an evening storm. Jake checked his watch and frowned. "Let's have a look at that niche."

They walked up to the second level and into the Argo section. Each wall held a series of niches, some just big enough to fit a funeral urn carved with the family name. Others were more ostentatious, a double or even triple size niche with a bigger casket. Many of the names were European in origin: Davenport, Schierholtz, Franklin. Some had pictures of the deceased, others held statuettes of angels or saints. One niche even had a Star of David carved into it. The Columbarium did not discriminate.

"Here it is." Jake stood in front of the Woodberry niche, a simple bronze urn behind a glass panel screwed into a wooden frame. He ran his fingers around the outside. "This looks simple enough to get off."

Morgan rifled through her pack and pulled out a multi-tool. Jake unscrewed the frame and placed it carefully on the floor. They reached in together to lift the giant urn down, heavy with the weight of ashes encased in thick metal. Morgan opened the lid and looked inside.

The thick grey powder of a human body reduced to dust half-filled the urn. A small chestnut-brown leather pouch etched with the cross and swirling wind rested on top.

"This has to be it! They interred his relic with him." Morgan reached in and carefully grasped the pouch. It was hard, and crackled as she lifted it out, tapping it gently against the edge of the urn to shake off the remaining ashes that clung to its base. She laid it on the top of her pack and began to pull on the ties that cinched the top.

Footsteps came from the entrance to the Columbarium.

Swiftly and silently, they lifted the urn back into the niche together. Jake held the glass up to the wooden panel, resting his head against it as if in mourning.

Morgan walked to the parapet, half-shielding him from view as Horace walked into the circular hall below.

"You folks alright up there? Need anything?"

Morgan waved and smiled. "We're fine, thanks." She glanced back at Jake and shrugged. "He's just a little overcome by the weight of history. We won't be too much longer."

Horace nodded, a sage expression on his old face. "You take your time now. I'll wait outside." He walked back out again.

"Some help here," Jake said through gritted teeth, his muscles straining with the weight of the glass. Morgan helped to support it as he stretched his arms out, then together, they screwed the pane back on again. The niche looked exactly as it always had.

Morgan knelt next to her pack and eased open the top of the pouch, Jake looking on with expectation as she revealed what was inside. A finger bone with the distinctive red seal.

Jake sighed with relief. "The last relic. That's all of them." He looked at his watch. "Just in time. We need to get ready for Alcatraz."

CHAPTER 23

MORGAN AND JAKE STOOD on the end of Pier 39 looking out toward Alcatraz. Lights still burned from the military fortification, a beacon in the dark bay. Behind them, the sound of tourists enjoying a night out, the roar of spectators watching football, and the buzz and ding of gaming machines. The smell of frying fish and the sweet scent of hot sugared doughnuts wafted on the breeze.

A sea lion barked from the floating platforms anchored in the protected bay nearby. Others joined in, their calls a warning in the night. Nature lived in uneasy partnership with humans here, their presence a draw for families while the wildlife was kept just far enough away so that the stink of their raft blew out to sea most days.

"The island is only two kilometers away," Jake said, "but we should probably leave soon." He reached for her hand. "I need to tell you something before we go."

Morgan turned to face him, the angles of his jawline lit by the strobe lights from one of the bars. His expression was somber, his eyes dark with intensity.

"Marietti wants the relics. We can't leave there without them."

"What about Naomi?"

"Well, obviously, we want her too. All three of us, plus

the Hand of Ezekiel, motoring back off Alcatraz in the early hours of the morning. That's the plan."

Morgan turned back to look out to sea. "What do you think the relics really are? If Marietti wants them that much, there must be something to the myth. Could they really raise the dead somehow?"

She thought of Ben in his grave, his body now becoming one with the earth, the creatures of the dirt crawling between his ribs, eating away the flesh that had been his shell for a short blink of time. The thought of someone opening his grave, pulling out his corpse and trying to make it live again was a sick perversion of the monk's belief in resurrection.

Jake leaned on the wooden ledge of the pier, his muscular forearms bronzed from the day's sun under his rolled-up shirt sleeves. "We've seen enough over the years to consider that anything is possible and certainly the Brotherhood have done a decent job of hiding the Hand of Ezekiel for generations. They must believe it has power." He shook his head. "I don't know. But aren't the relics better off in the ARKANE vault, safe from crazy billionaires who want to conquer death?"

"Perhaps." Morgan hefted her pack over her shoulder, the remaining finger bones safely stowed inside. "Let's go bring Naomi home."

They walked along the side of the pier down to the moorings. Masts creaked in the wind, the metallic clatter of rigging on the yachts and the slap of water on the side of the wharf welcoming them onto the dock. They searched for the launch Martin had arranged for them to use.

"There it is." Jake pointed at a Sea Ray Sundancer moored at the end of the row. As they climbed aboard, Morgan noted the name of the boat.

"Boreas. Seriously? The god of the north wind who brings the winter. Couldn't we have got something with a more triumphant name?"

Jake stowed the gear, fitting their packs under removable panels in the seats. He opened up a waterproof bag that had been left for them. "This might help you feel better."

Morgan bent to look inside, noting her favorite SP-21 Barak pistol next to a selection of other weapons. She nodded, then looked up at the busy pier above them, noting the tourists that wandered with carefree nonchalance along the walkway. "I'll check it all once we get underway."

She untied the main line from the back, and Jake eased the powerboat into the channel, chugging slowly until they reached the entrance to the small harbor.

"Hold on," he called back to Morgan and then powered into the bay, turning the boat into a wide arc, heading northwest toward Alcatraz. Above them in the night sky, the clouds darkened to shades of mulberry shot through with inky black, heavy with rain as the storm approached.

The wind whipped through Morgan's hair, and she relished the sting of salt spray on her skin as they sped away from the city toward the forbidding island. She felt the edge of adrenalin rise as they skimmed the waves, the twin poles of apprehension and excitement. The throb of her burns seemed to lessen as she focused on the task. This was where she was meant to be – out on a mission, her partner by her side, set against the enemy together. She couldn't help the smile that curved over her face and she knew that Father Ben would have approved of her choice to rejoin the fray.

The lighthouse blinked from the center of the island and the white blocks of the prison loomed above as they drew closer. Jake slowed the boat as they approached the shore, idling the engine as they both checked their weapons and hid backups. Morgan tucked a ceramic blade into a compartment in the base of her hiking boots.

Jake looked at his watch, the minutes ticking toward midnight. "Ready?"

Morgan nodded. "As I'll ever be."

They moored the boat around the coastline from the pier, tying up to a small jetty at the base of the Agave Trail, a walkway through sharp spiky succulents that wound up to the prison beyond. The lone cry of a Western Gull rang through the air like a desperate call for help. It circled above, beady eyes fixed on the intruders as it hovered in the rising wind.

Morgan and Jake grabbed their packs and clambered onto the island, creeping up the flagstone steps to the ruins of the parade ground. They emerged behind a pile of rubble, woven through with weeds and scrub grass, nature claiming back the concrete inch by inch. They looked up toward the prison on the cell-house slope above, the burned-out ruins of the Warden's residence visible next to the lighthouse.

"Where are we meant to do the exchange?" Morgan said softly.

Jake pointed to the side of the rocky outcrop where a long ramp led into the shadows. "There's a morgue on the north-western side near the water tower. We meet there."

As they walked with quiet steps around the edge of the abandoned parade ground, Morgan looked up at the prison, trying to imagine what it must have been like to be incarcerated here surrounded by the stark waters of the bay. It had been a military prison since 1828 and a federal prison from the 1930s until 1963, later becoming a historical landmark visited by tourists fascinated by the lore of the inescapable rock.

But it wasn't only history that made this place so forbidding. As Morgan gazed at the stone walls, she felt a chill that went beyond history. The Native Americans called this place an evil island, and the violent inmates had certainly brought more brutality with them. The earth had soaked up the blood and tears of those within, and the air seemed to resonate with the frustrated screams of those trapped here until death, and the echoes of those they had wronged.

Aware of the silence around them, Morgan and Jake walked up the slope to the tiny morgue. It was little more than a concrete bunker with a thick door, rusting on its hinges with a glass panel allowing a view inside. Morgan rubbed away a layer of dirt and peered in, her flashlight illuminating a ruined interior. The faded white brickwork was layered with dust and peeled off the walls revealing bricks beneath. A single wooden table, the length of a man, stood off-center, grooves still visible where liquids from the corpse would have pooled. Broken pipes and crumpled plumbing lay in the corner.

The sound of hydraulics suddenly came from within, the whirr of a turbine, the clatter of a chain.

A door opened at the back of the morgue, brightly lit from within, and Morgan recognized the muscle-bound frame of the Latino military man she'd first seen in Toledo. A semi-automatic hung around one broad shoulder. He held the barrel toward them as he pressed a button and the morgue door clicked and swung open.

"Leave your weapons here." His voice was curt, his expression stony.

Morgan and Jake stepped into the morgue and laid their guns on the table.

"And the rest." The man's tone was clear, so Morgan and Jake both pulled their backup guns from ankle holsters and laid them next to the others.

"In the elevator, face the back wall. Hands where I can see them."

They did as he said. The elevator was pristine, sparkling clean with chrome surfaces so shiny that Morgan could see the man's reflection. As the door shut, he pressed another button to descend, keeping the gun on them at all times.

Morgan turned her head slightly toward Jake, catching his eye. They exchanged a silent gaze, both understanding that they would wait to see how to proceed further. There had been no underground part of the prison on Martin's maps, but somehow it didn't seem surprising that there was a hidden place of secrets under this highly protected site.

The elevator descended, halting with a bump at the bottom. The chrome door slid open with a whoosh. The Latino guard stepped out first, backing away, his gun trained on them the whole time. "Out. Turn around slowly."

They turned, and Morgan couldn't help but gasp at what lay in front of them.

CHAPTER 24

Morgan had expected some kind of historic dungeon, but this was a state-of-the-art medical research lab. They had known of Luis Rey's ties to the military but what he did here must be directly under the auspices of government, and only a stone's throw from the Silicon Valley billionaires who chased immortality at any price.

The lab was compact, the ceiling low and hung with silver ventilation ducts and metallic pipes. Morgan didn't know what most of the medical equipment was for, but that wasn't what caught her eye.

On one side of the room, a row of four bodies lay on metal gurneys, three male, one female, all young, all strapped down and all showing signs of violent death. They had been shot in the head recently. Powerful vents whooshed as they conditioned the air but the room still smelled of a hint of smoke and underneath it, a note of decay. Morgan noticed that the gunshot wounds had not bled and two of the bodies showed signs of decomposition. It looked like they had been shot after death – but surely, that couldn't be right.

Behind the gurneys, a barred door led into a darkened cell. On the other side of the room, screened off from the dead by a green surgical curtain, a Creole scientist with blue beads in her hair stood tapping on a computer tablet, checking readings on a monitor. In front of her, a young girl lay in a hospital bed, her body twisted, her face pale and sweating with pain even though she was under sedation. The regular beep of the machine traced the pulse of the girl's life.

"You took Naomi from the bayou." Jake started toward the woman, fists clenched. "Lashonda, right?"

At the sound of his voice, a rattling came from the cell beyond, and a face appeared. Naomi stood there, hands around the metal bars. She wore a white hospital gown as if prepped for an operation. Her skin was sallow, her wrists raw from the shackles but her eyes were still bright with curiosity.

"Jake? You're really here!"

"Naomi!" Jake stepped forward, heading toward the cell.

The bodyguard stopped him with a sharp dig in the ribs with his gun. "No further."

Lashonda regarded the newcomers with calculated interest. "Did you bring the relics?" She pointed at the girl in the bed. "Elena doesn't have much time." She looked over at the bodyguard. "Julio, take the bag."

"It's OK, I'll do it." Morgan shrugged off her pack, her hands in clear view so Julio wouldn't get trigger-happy.

She pushed it gently with her foot, sliding it forward. Lashonda walked over, bent to pick it up, and carried it over to one of the metal tables. She ran a detection wand over it with a light beeping noise. "It's clear."

"Of course it is," Morgan said. "There are only bones in there. Now let Naomi out of the cell and let us leave."

Something about the place made her skin crawl, and she had a dark sense of foreboding. They needed to get off this forsaken island of violence and death. Let Marietti return for the relics himself. It would be a win if they could just get themselves out alive tonight.

"But surely you must want to know what the Hand of Ezekiel can do." The voice came from a doorway behind Elena's hospital bed.

A Hispanic man stood curved over an ebony walking cane, twisted fingers grasping the bone handle. His face was scored with deep wrinkles, aged before his time by the disease that ravaged his body but there was a core of steel beneath. From the research Martin had provided, Morgan realized that this must be Luis Rey, the billionaire who would try to conquer even death to save his daughter.

"I know what you do at ARKANE," he said. "So you must be curious. Can the relics really turn dry bone to living flesh once more?" The beep of Elena's machine filled the brief silence, the blip of an erratic heartbeat as Luis looked down upon her prone body.

He pointed over to the dead lying on the gurneys beyond. "We've tried so many variations of the powder but there has always been something missing. Something that perhaps the relics will provide. Something that will bring Elena back."

Morgan looked over at Jake. He shook his head almost imperceptibly, and she cursed his need to fulfill the mission, to retrieve the relics as well as Naomi. She trusted him enough to follow through with whatever he had in mind, but she felt the threatening edge of her own weakness lying beneath that certainty.

Luis nodded at Lashonda. She opened the pack, pulling out the packages that held the finger bones. Morgan found herself holding her breath in anticipation. These relics had not been together for centuries and whatever the truth of their mythological power, they had been protected for generations. Was the Hand of Ezekiel really of God, or was it from the darkness?

Lashonda laid the finger bones on a workbench, and for a moment, Morgan thought they were free and clear. They could just walk out with Naomi and make it back to San Francisco for a late-night drink.

But then everything changed.

Luis bent to examine the bone from Lima. He looked up

sharply, his eyes blazing with anger. "This one is empty. It's a shell. The powder inside is missing."

Jake shrugged. "It was in a pile of bones in the lost chambers of a catacomb. We were lucky to even find it."

Luis thumped his fist on the table, shaking the other relics. "It's not enough. You'll pay for the failure. We need more test subjects, and she will be the first."

He turned toward Naomi, but Jake didn't even wait for the end of the sentence. He moved fast, spinning low, ducking under Julio's arm. He thrust up hard, knocking the barrel of the gun up and away.

Julio shot off a couple of rounds. Luis ducked and pulled Lashonda down with him as bullets pinged off the metallic pipes above.

A sudden hissing sound filled the room as one burst. Water sprayed out, dripping down the walls.

Morgan dove sideways, rolling to her feet, pulling the ceramic knife from her boot, yanking back Julio's throat as Jake pinned his arm. She held the blade at his jugular. "Easy now."

Jake took the gun off him and pointed it at Luis and Lashonda cowering on the floor. "Now we're going to do this my way."

A moment of silence, then a voice, reedy and weak.

"Jake."

Naomi stood against the bars, one hand clutched against her chest. Red blood soaked through her gown where two bullets had torn into her. She sank to her knees, eyes closing as she collapsed.

"No!" Jake shouted.

His distraction gave Julio an opening. The big bodyguard thrust both fists behind him, raking his fingers down Morgan's burned legs. She howled and backed away, explosions of white-hot pain wracking her body as she dropped to the ground, clutching at her thighs, breath fast.

Julio snatched for the weapon.

Jake spun back toward him, enraged. He used the butt of the gun to whip Julio on the side of his head, knocking the man to the ground, taking his rage out on the bodyguard even as Julio fought back.

The men tussled, sliding through the water that dripped onto the floor from the leaking pipes, but Jake's anger drove him harder. He straddled the bodyguard, punching him over and over –

The high-pitched whine of an alarm filled the room. Elena's monitor. Her heartbeat had stopped.

"No!" Luis shuffled over to his little girl's bedside, Lashonda ahead of him.

She checked the monitors, grabbed defibrillator paddles. She paused with them over the little girl's chest. "This is the fourth time tonight. She can't take much more."

Luis urged her on as tears streamed down his face. "Do it, please. Don't let her go."

Lashonda placed the paddles and shocked the tiny body. The monitor flared into life again but then died. She pressed the button again.

Morgan watched from the floor in a haze of pain. As they worked on the little girl in desperation, she finally understood why this broken man was willing to risk everything, perhaps even eternal damnation, to keep his daughter alive.

Jake held Julio down with a bloody fist and punched him hard one more time. As the bodyguard slumped in a daze, Jake ran over to Naomi in the cell.

He touched her hand. "Hold on now, we're getting you out of here."

Naomi looked up at him, her arm clutching her chest as blood pooled around her.

"It's too late," she whispered, reaching up and stroking Jake's cheek. Then she gazed across the room at Elena. "Save her …"

Naomi's arm dropped, and her head lolled to one side. Jake reached through the bars, pulling her to him.

At that moment, Elena's monitor flatlined, and from where she lay, Morgan saw the shadow of death lengthen in front of her, while those who fought against it stood like Ezekiel pleading with the Lord for one last breath.

"There's still a chance," Lashonda said, once again the cool-headed scientist. "I'm almost there with the formula. The last batch was so close. Perhaps one of these bones contains the missing element."

"Test them," Luis said, his eyes glazed as he looked down at his daughter. "Do it. Now."

Lashonda went to the table where the relics lay. She gathered them up and carried them over to her lab bench. Morgan watched as the scientist used a syringe to plunge through the wax of the most intact finger bone and extract some of what lay within.

"I've already synthesized a formula based on Haitian voodoo and records gathered from West Africa." Lashonda placed the off-white powder in a vial and shook it. "But something was missing. I used it on batches of test subjects, and some came back, but they were raving, they were animals. We had to ..." She pointed beyond the curtain to the dead bodies on the gurneys. "So, there has to be something else."

She placed the vial in a mass spectrometer and began the analysis of the bone powder. "This will take a few minutes, and then I can compare the samples. Find the differential." Her eyes flicked over to Naomi in the cell. "Then I need to test the batch."

Jake whirled around, his eyes blazing in anger. "No. You can't use her that way. It's not what she would have wanted ..."

His words trailed off and Morgan saw realization dawn on his face. Naomi's outstretched arm still reached toward Elena and her last words had been for the little girl.

Luis pulled a bunch of keys from his pocket. "They spent time together in the last days," he said softly. "Naomi spoke of her lost sister."

He threw the keys over to Jake. "Here, lift her out and help me move them both into the resurrection room back here."

Jake caught the keys and stood for a moment looking down at them.

Then he straightened up and unlocked Naomi's cell, pulling her from within. He lifted her prone body, and she lolled in his arms, her blood soaking through his shirt. Morgan pushed down the pain in her legs and pulled herself up, following them into the resurrection room.

It was shadowed inside with the sweet smell of incense in the air, a far cry from the bright lights of the medical lab beyond. This was a place of worship, a place where the saints could intercede for the living. But the smell of the dead was here too and in the glimmer of candlelight, Morgan noticed stains on the floor, offerings to an ancient god who demanded blood sacrifice. The bodies on the gurneys had been shot in here, executed when they had returned as something less than human.

A thick scarlet candle stood on a plain stone altar, casting flickering shadows over the silver box that lay open on top. The box of bone they had only seen in pictures, the box that completed the Hand of Ezekiel.

Luis laid Elena down on one of the gurneys. He tucked a blanket around her, and even as tears streamed down his face, he shackled her tiny wrists to the metal frame. His hands shook, his eyes never leaving her.

Jake placed Naomi's body down on another gurney next to the little girl, her face just as innocent, her skin barely marked with a wrinkle. Morgan reached out and checked Naomi's pulse, but she already knew there was nothing left in this earthly shell. She had not known the woman in life, but she was a fellow agent, and deserved better than this accidental death on a cursed island.

She looked at Jake. "Did she believe?"

He nodded. "Her faith never encroached on her work at ARKANE. Somehow she managed to reconcile both worlds." He sighed. "More than I could ever do, that's for sure."

Lashonda rushed into the room. "I think I found something."

CHAPTER 25

"I TESTED ALL THE bones, and there's an element common to all that I missed in the first stage." Lashonda held up a test tube containing a thick paste. "But I think this will work."

She took a step toward Naomi, but Jake stopped her, his hand against her chest. "Oh, no. You're not using her as a lab rat. Try it out on Elena."

Tears ran down Luis's face as he reached out with a shaking hand. "She's all I have left. Please."

Morgan took a deep breath. "What would Naomi have done?"

Jake thumped a fist into his open hand then exhaled sharply. "She would have volunteered herself rather than hurt a little girl." He backed away from the bench, handed Morgan the gun. "But I can't ... do what might be necessary."

Lashonda walked to the side of the gurney with the mixture. Morgan stood opposite her holding Naomi's hand. As she looked into the scientist's sapphire eyes, she saw a glimmer of darkness, like the writhing coils of a sea-serpent underneath calm waters. How many lives had this woman taken in pursuit of conquering death? How many more would she be willing to sacrifice?

Lashonda spooned some of the paste from the test tube.

Doubt clouded Morgan's mind, and she put a hand out to stop the scientist.

"Wait. There must be a reason why it's called the Hand of Ezekiel. If it was just some relic paste, why call it the Hand?"

Lashonda held the spoon to Naomi's lips. "It's only a legend. Means nothing."

Morgan pushed the spoon away, covering Naomi's mouth. "Myths always have a grain of truth in them. Faith and science wind together like strands of DNA. They're inseparable."

"She's right." Luis's voice was tired, as if he carried a great weight in his soul. "In my family journals, there's a passage about the Hand, about words said over the corpse so it might rise."

"I'll get the relics." Jake dashed out into the main room.

He returned quickly with the finger bones, but as he swung through the door, a wash of water came with him. It smelled of brackish sea water and an edge of industrial oil. "It's flooding in there, but slowly, so we have a little time."

Morgan took the box of bone from the altar and opened the intricate lid. Together, she and Jake fitted the bone relics into the box so they stood tall, five fingers of five saints, those who believed the dead could truly rise.

"Now what?" Jake asked.

Morgan carried the box and placed it on Naomi's chest. "We prophesy as Ezekiel did." She nodded at Lashonda and the scientist spooned the paste into Naomi's mouth, rubbing it over her full lips.

Morgan spoke the words of Ezekiel. "Come, breath, from the four winds and breathe into these slain, that they may live."

She knew the words of Jewish scripture by heart, an allegory of the nation of Israel who had turned away from God. But could it possibly be more than that?

Would such words work when spoken by someone who

doubted, even though she had seen miracles in the fires of Pentecost and darkness within the Gates of Hell?

Morgan spoke again, stronger this time. "Come, breath, from the four winds and breathe into these slain, that they may live."

Naomi lay still, her skin cooling, the paste a white mush on the bow of her mouth. No breath stirred her.

Lashonda hung her head. "This can't be right. I'll try another formula."

Suddenly, a far-off rumble echoed through the room, the storm finally overhead. Then the ground shook, and a rushing sound came from the lab beyond.

Jake turned to the door and yanked it open, letting in another wash of water. "We need to get out of here. The flood is rising. This place will be underwater in a few minutes."

"Wait." Morgan pointed at Naomi's foot. It twitched for a second time and then she felt pressure on her fingers. "Something's happening."

She moved the box of relics back to the altar.

Jake pushed Lashonda to one side so he could get closer. "Naomi?" His voice held a note of hope.

Naomi's eyes flickered a little and then she opened them. Morgan looked down at her, seeing gold flecks in the chestnut hue as Naomi blinked with confusion. For a moment, Morgan saw life there, intelligence, humanity – then it was as if a sandstorm blew across, a tempest in the desert sweeping away all before it, scouring life from its path.

Naomi's top lip curled and she bared her teeth as she snarled, her fingers curving into talons. She raked at the air. She writhed on the gurney, pulling at her restraints, rattling her chains, straining muscles that tightened with every movement.

Morgan and Jake stepped back out of her reach, waiting, hoping that somehow the real Naomi might come back.

Lashonda shook her head. "This is what happened before.

Something is still wrong with the formula." She looked over at Luis as he bent over his daughter. "I can fix this. I can try again."

Jake wiped his eyes, then his expression hardened into anger. "Maybe there's nothing wrong with the formula. Maybe that's what an army of the dead looks like."

His words struck Morgan's heart with a measure of truth. There was no resurrection in this life, there was no rising from the dead until the End Times, and those who sought to conquer death would find only the taste of ashes in their mouths.

The sound of rushing water grew louder, the flooding now around their ankles.

Jake looked at the grunting animal that had once been Naomi Locasto. "We need to let her go and get out of here."

Morgan nodded. "I'll do it. Go see to Julio. I'll only be a minute."

Jake sighed and went to the door, taking one last look at Naomi, then he walked out into the ever-deeper water.

Morgan felt the chill of the flood as it crept up her legs, covering her inflamed burns, numbing her wounds for one glorious moment. Then she realized that it was part of her now, and pain meant that she was still alive.

She looked down at the former ARKANE agent. "We'll remember you," she whispered. "We'll look after your family."

Morgan held the gun to Naomi's forehead and pulled the trigger, the harsh sound a final violation. The body lay still, finally at peace.

Lashonda turned to Luis. "Let me try one more variation. I have an idea that might just work. We can bring Elena back."

Morgan held up her gun, pointing it at the back of Lashonda's head. Something in the scientist's eyes had given her a glimpse of a world to come. She would never stop pursuing this research, she would not give up her quest for immortality. This lab would be underwater soon, drowning the research, but Lashonda would remember it. She would take it to another billionaire, another off-the-radar lab. The dead would rise again, and next time, there might not be anyone to stop her. Morgan couldn't let that happen.

Luis stared back at his scientist, looking as if he was only one step from the grave himself. But Morgan also saw a spark of realization in his eyes. He knew it was the end.

Luis shook his head. "No more. If Elena cannot rise, then no one else will either. It ends here."

With one smooth movement, he raised his arm, gun in hand, and shot Lashonda in the head at close range. Her body dropped heavily, floating in the rising waters as blood pooled around her.

Morgan stood silently, her own weapon pointing at Luis as he held his gun out toward her. A moment passed as their eyes met.

Then he blinked, dropped his arm, turned back to Elena. Morgan slowly lowered her weapon. Luis was now a broken man, his ambitions ended, his family line finished. He climbed onto his daughter's bed, wrapped his arms around her and closed his eyes, waiting for the waters to cover them both.

Morgan grabbed the box of bones from the altar and waded through the flood back into the lab. Sparks flashed from equipment overhead as lights faded in and out.

Jake stood at an open emergency stairwell by the elevator, a still-woozy Julio by his side. Morgan lifted the box higher as she crossed the lab, the water now chest-height. Jake helped her out of the flood, and they began to climb away from the doomed lab and up to the main island above.

They emerged from the emergency tunnel on the outside of the morgue. Rain lashed down as thunder rolled overhead, lightning slashing the sky into shards.

Jake pushed open the door to the morgue and cuffed Julio to the old table where he might be found in the morning.

"I didn't know he would take it that far." The bodyguard's eyes were haunted. He shook his head. "I'm Catholic. I know the dead should only rise in the End Times. Is he –?"

Morgan nodded. "He died next to Elena."

Julio hung his head. "That's how it should be. Thank you."

They left him there in darkness as the storm raged about them, and together, Morgan and Jake ran back toward the parade ground. The pain in Morgan's legs arced through her as she pushed on through the rain but now it felt like a blessing, a promise of life, a feeling of renewal as her skin sought to heal.

They reached the edge of the parade ground as the rain began to ease. As they stood together looking out across the bay, it was as if they were alone in the world. Fog hung over the water, a dense cloud that blocked everything from sight, deadening sound. There were shadows out there in the gloom, strange shapes with claws and teeth and scales, wandering souls amid the haunting cry of seabirds.

Morgan looked down at the engraved box of bones.

"No one should have these. We can't take them back." She dropped to her knees and placed the box on the ground. She opened it and pulled out the finger bones, laying them on the rock. She picked up a lump of concrete and lifted it high, ready to smash it down.

"Wait." Jake stopped her, holding her arm away from the relics. "The ARKANE vault is full of such artifacts. Why are these any different?"

Morgan looked up, her thoughts with Ben. "You saw what Naomi became. If these can really raise an army of the dead, an army of those – things – then they must be destroyed. The dead should stay in the grave."

Jake nodded, then dropped to his knees beside her. "And with the relics gone, then the Brotherhood of the Breath have nothing further to protect. They can fade into history along with the Inquisition that spawned them." He picked up another piece of concrete. "I'll help you."

Together, they smashed the relics into powder, turning the bones into tiny fragments. The gentle rain washed the remains into the debris of the parade ground and down over the Agave Trail, fertilizing new life on the cursed island, as dawn rose over the city beyond.

* * *

THE END

ENJOYED VALLEY OF DRY BONES?

If you loved the book and have a moment to spare, I would really appreciate a short review on the page where you bought the book. Your help in spreading the word is gratefully appreciated and reviews make a huge difference to helping new readers find the series. Thank you!

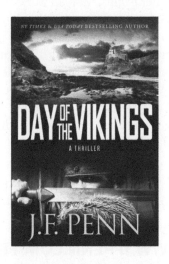

Get a free copy of the bestselling thriller, *Day of the Vikings*, ARKANE book 5, when you sign up to join my Reader's Group. You'll also be notified of new releases, giveaways and receive personal updates from behind the scenes of my thrillers.

WWW.JFPENN.COM/FREE

* * *

Day of the Vikings, an ARKANE thriller

A ritual murder on a remote island under the shifting skies of the aurora borealis.

A staff of power that can summon Ragnarok, the Viking apocalypse.

When Neo-Viking terrorists invade the British Museum in London to reclaim the staff of Skara Brae, ARKANE agent Dr. Morgan Sierra is trapped in the building along with hostages under mortal threat.

As the slaughter begins, Morgan works alongside psychic Blake Daniel to discern the past of the staff, dating back to islands invaded by the Vikings generations ago.

Can Morgan and Blake uncover the truth before Ragnarok is unleashed, consuming all in its wake?

Day of the Vikings is a fast-paced, supernatural thriller set in London and the islands of Orkney, Lindisfarne and Iona. Set in the present day, it resonates with the history and myth of the Vikings.

If you love an action-packed thriller,
you can get Day of the Vikings for free now:

WWW.JFPENN.COM/FREE

Day of the Vikings features Dr. Morgan Sierra from the ARKANE thrillers, and Blake Daniel from the London Crime Thrillers, but it is also a stand-alone novella that can be read and enjoyed separately.

AUTHOR'S NOTE

As with all my novels, this story is based on my travels and the history and characters I find along the way. It turned out to be quite different to what I had originally planned. Sometimes, that's just the way it happens! I like to write a story that is based on truth and then twist it into fiction and this time, even I was surprised by what I discovered in my research.

The seed of the idea was planted when I visited New Orleans in 2017. While wandering around the city, I discovered the copy of the Toledo Bible at the back of St Louis Cathedral and learned about the links to the Spanish Inquisition through the painting of Père Antoine in the Cabildo next door. I did a voodoo tour of the city and St Louis cemetery No. 1 and a story idea started to form. I've always loved the Valley of Dry Bones chapter in the book of Ezekiel and it seemed to fit with the zombies of voodoo – and from there, I started down the rabbit hole of research.

You can see a collection of images from my research at: www.pinterest.com/jfpenn/valley-of-dry-bones

The history of the Spanish Empire

Many people know New Orleans has a French Quarter but the Spanish influence is not so well-known. As I looked into the history of the Empire, I discovered the link with Equatorial Guinea in West Africa, an area that also has links with voodoo. It seemed plausible that these traditions became entwined through the forced movement of people through the slave trade.

After researching how the Spanish Catholics colonized the New World, I learned how they had also settled in the Philippines and Peru at the same time and that many of the monks came from the same ecclesiastical colleges.

Spain

I went to Toledo in 2018 to see the original St Louis Bible, and while it doesn't have a *hamsa* in it, the history of the Jewish community in the city is mostly correct.

The relic room in the old house is based on the Monastery of the Incarnation, which is actually in Madrid. We endured a tour in Spanish that focused primarily on some terrible artwork before finally being led into the relic room that was the highlight of the tour. It is incredible, well-worth a visit if you are in the city and a little obsessed with bones, as I am!

Bruegel's *Triumph of Death* was on display in the Prado when I visited in 2018, and we had some wonderful *tapas* at La Musa Latina in Palacio De Los Vargas along with some local Ribera.

When visiting Majorca a month later, our hotel happened to be right around the corner from the Basilica of San Francesc and the statue of Junípero Serra, the kind of synchronicity that I am used to experiencing on book research trips. If you keep an open mind while you travel, these things tend to happen! Since I had visited the Mission

Dolores in San Francisco a year prior, and seen Serra's relic, this enabled me to further tie the story together.

As ever, Morgan's impressions are my own, and I fell in love with the old city of Palma. The cathedral really does have a Gaudí *baldachin* and a statue of a winged skeleton which I was thrilled to find in a chapel near the back if you happen to visit.

You can find my pictures from Madrid, Toledo and Palma, Majorca at: www.jfpenn.com/spain2018

New Orleans and voodoo

Père Antoine was Grand Inquisitor at St Louis Cathedral. The painting mentioned in the Cabildo is the *Portrait of Père Antoine (Padre Antonio de Sedella) at Age Seventy-Four*, by Edmund Brewster, New Orleans, 1822. I'm not sure what the book is on the table, but it's definitely too thin to be the entire Bible. Perhaps it is indeed the book of Ezekiel?

I did two fantastic trips into Jean Lafitte National Historical Park and Preserve: the first on an airboat where we had some up close experiences with alligators; the other by kayak through the backwaters of the bayou, which was just magical.

I met some wonderful people in New Orleans who showed me how much voodoo is entwined with Catholicism, so I hope my respect for tradition in clear in the story. The ceremony in the bayou is based on details in *The Serpent and the Rainbow* by Wade Davis, and also episode 7 of season 1 of *Dark Tourist* on Netflix which was about voodoo in Benin.

You can find my pictures from New Orleans and the bayou at: www.JFPenn.com/nolapics

Technology and bio-technology

The digitalization of the Vatican Archives is an ongoing project. You can find all the details at: digi.vatlib.it

Fibrodysplasia ossificans progressiva is a real medical condition which causes fibrous tissue to ossify spontaneously or when damaged.

Human longevity is being funded by billionaires in Silicon Valley. Calico Labs is backed by Alphabet (Google's parent company). Human Longevity Inc was founded by Craig Venter who was involved with sequencing the first human genome, and Peter Diamandis, founder of the X-Prize, whose stated goal is to live to for 700 years. You can get a transfusion of young blood from Ambrosia Medical, who are opening their first clinic in New York at the end of 2018. The Methuselah Foundation has a goal of making 90 the new 50 by 2030.

There was a debate at the Vatican in May 2018 about the Morality of Immortality. Rabbi Dr. Edward Reichman gave a biblical perspective on aging, noting that Methuselah lived to 969 years old.

When Morgan is thinking about death, she quotes from Dylan Thomas's poem, *Do not go gentle into that good night*.

San Francisco

I visited San Francisco in 2017 and loved the Columbarium so much that it had to go in the book. I took some liberties with what it contains, but it is indeed kept in meticulous condition by Emmitt Watson, the cheerful African-American caretaker I met. His office is filled with photos of visitors and he told me some fantastic stories about the experiences he has had there over the years. He even has a comic about him, *The Palace of Ashes* by Andy Warner.

The details of Mission Dolores are based on my visit

there and it is true that Junípero Serra's relics were dispersed based on donations. His canonization was contested by Native American groups but went ahead in September 2015. The journalist and historian, Carey McWilliams, described the Missions as 'a series of picturesque charnel houses.'

Alcatraz does have a small morgue but the underground chamber is my own embellishment.

You can find my pictures from San Francisco at: www.JFPenn.com/sfpics

I've also written an article about the strange places I found at: www.JFPenn.com/unusual-san-francisco

Any mistakes in the research that are not intentional for fictional purposes are my own.

ACKNOWLEDGMENTS

To my readers – thank you for returning to another ARKANE adventure. I thought Morgan had retired for good after End of Days, but you encouraged me to bring her back, and there are more adventures to come!

Thanks to Jen Blood, my fantastic first reader and story editor, for her continued insights. Thanks to Wendy Janes for another great proofread.

Thanks to my beta readers: Laura and Dan Martone at TheMartones.com for expertise on New Orleans, Kristen Tate at TheBlueGarret.com for San Francisco notes, and to Samantha Keel at ScriptMedicBlog.com for vetting Morgan's injuries and for helping me understand character motivation from a different point of view.

Thanks also to Bruce Beck who told me about the keys handed down through generations of Toledo Jews.

Thanks to Jane Dixon Smith at JDSmith-Design.com for the great cover design and print formatting.

MORE BOOKS BY J.F.PENN

Thanks for joining Morgan, Jake and the
ARKANE team. The adventures continue …

Stone of Fire #1
Crypt of Bone #2
Ark of Blood #3
One Day in Budapest #4
Day of the Vikings #5
Gates of Hell #6
One Day in New York #7
Destroyer of Worlds #8
End of Days #9
Valley of Dry Bones #10

If you like **crime thrillers with an edge of the supernatural**,
join Detective Jamie Brooke and museum researcher Blake
Daniel, in the London Crime Thriller trilogy:

Desecration #1
Delirium #2
Deviance #3

If you enjoy **dark fantasy,** check out:

Map of Shadows, Mapwalkers #1
Risen Gods
American Demon Hunters: Sacrifice

A Thousand Fiendish Angels:
Short stories based on Dante's Inferno

The Dark Queen

More books coming soon.

You can sign up to be notified of new releases, giveaways
and pre-release specials - plus, get a free book!

WWW.JFPENN.COM/FREE

ABOUT J.F.PENN

J.F.Penn is the Award-nominated, New York Times and USA Today bestselling author of the ARKANE supernatural thrillers, London Crime Thrillers, and the Mapwalker dark fantasy series, as well as other standalone stories.

Her books weave together ancient artifacts, relics of power, international locations and adventure with an edge of the supernatural. Joanna lives in Bath, England and enjoys a nice G&T.

* * *

You can sign up for a free thriller,
Day of the Vikings, and updates from behind the scenes,
research, and giveaways at:

WWW.JFPENN.COM/FREE

* * *

Connect at:
www.JFPenn.com
joanna@JFPenn.com
www.Facebook.com/JFPennAuthor
www.Instagram.com/JFPennAuthor
www.Twitter.com/JFPennWriter

* * *

For writers:

Joanna's site, www.TheCreativePenn.com, helps people write, publish and market their books through articles, audio, video and online courses.

She writes non-fiction for authors under Joanna Penn and has an award-nominated podcast for writers, The Creative Penn Podcast.

ND - #0289 - 290823 - C0 - 203/127/13 - PB - 9781912105175 - Matt Lamination